A true story in part, and an alarming message to America in whole

MARLINS CRY

A Phishing Story

The Digital Damnation
of Civilized Society

A Battle Cry for Cyber Security
For Individuals and
The Business World's Big Fish

By Casey Tennyson Swann

A gripping novel exposing the potent potential of peril
caused by spyware on a single phone
and electronic espionage of major entities

COPYRIGHT

Title:
Marlins Cry
A Phishing Story
The Digital Damnation of Civilized Society

Published by:
Cutting Edge Communications, Inc.
P.O. Box 476, Winter Park, FL 32790 USA

Written by:
Casey Tennyson Swann

Copyright:
2012 Cutting Edge Communications, Inc.

Printed in USA

International Standard Book Number
ISBN number 978-0-9883993-0-3

Other books by Author Casey Tennyson Swann:

Lessons From A Falling Leaf
Secrets Of The Southern Shells
Bait For Fish Bigger Than I Am
Marlins Cry A Phishing Story

And others on
www.CaseyCreates.com

INTRODUCTION

THE STORY takes place marlin fishing on a boat in the Bahamas, with a main character, a writer, who is victimized by spyware. She relives her terror daydreaming on the boat. The boat owner, her PR firm client, is being attacked by corporate electronic espionage that threatens demise for the whole country. The boat captain, and several other characters, all receive the plight of the two victims with varying degrees of interest, mostly indifference. The story outlines a wake up call for America to protect itself, because we are all connected, starting with responsibility of each individual who uses a phone or computer. The story softens the fear factor with a spiritual message of hope.

THE GIST of the book is best summarized by the main character in Chapter 12:
"I am afraid that my stalker might kill me, yes, but my bigger fear is that our entire civilized society, as we know it and enjoy it, is in terrible jeopardy. Unscrupulous international criminal minds can wipe out our infrastructure and bring us to a third-world scavenger survival-mode. They can do it in an instant, totally invisible and virtually untraceable, from anywhere in the world."

THE INSPIRATION was from a real experience highlighted by a few key digital messages. Details were added which are fiction.

Real 6/12/11 as spyware was being researched and resolved:

The screen savers showed Word-of-the-day dictionary messages. I read them aloud to (Owen).

"Attenuate. Verb. Reduce the force, effect or value of. Reduce the amplitude of such as of a signal, electrical current, or other oscillation. Adj. Attenuated. Reduce the virulence of such as of a pathogenic organism or vaccine. Reduce in thickness. Make thin."

Another screen popped up and I read it aloud, "Wrath. Noun. Extreme anger chiefly used for humorous or rhetorical effect."

Another screen saver popped up as I finished reading that one and again, I read it aloud, "Westering. Adj. especially of the sun nearing the west."

"Oh my God! Is this a threat? Am I in danger? This has to stop! Help me," I cried out to (Owen) on the phone.

Real 6/6/12, a year later, written as notes for *Marlins Cry* book were dusted from a storage box, and the first few pages of a year old InDesign document were loaded from a USB drive to a new Mac:

The message on the computer screen read, "ef.fi.ca.cious Adjective: Successful in producing a desired or intended result; effective. Synonyms: effective – effectual – efficient – operative – potent."

CONTENTS

INTRODUCTION

CHAPTERS

AUTHOR'S NOTE

CHAPTER 1, DIGITAL DETOX LAST JULY

The tangerine sun crept over the crests of the pines painting a pastel panorama of peaceful hues rainbow-ing through the fog. I hadn't seen much of the outside world since May. I put my windows down to smell the fresh scent of nurturing Mother Nature. The soft colors of the horizon soothed the blood shot eyes from the sting of days spent glaring at computer monitors. The ice cream stand sandwiched between miles of lush farmlands, green houses and dairy pastures reminded me that there is life outside of my business. The iconic peaceful images could be photographed for *Time*. A boiled peanut trailer lay sleeping on the side of State Road 44 beside the dew glistened white fireworks tent.

Shockingly, like a surreal scene from Blair Witch Project, an emotional fireworks explosion burst inside the car. The radio awakened my heightened senses to the words of Adele and *Rolling In The Deep*. The jarring lyrics, "There's a fire starting in my heart, Reaching a fever pitch, And it's bringing me out of the dark ..."

When it sang, "You're gonna' wish you had never met me..." I freaked out and hit the off button to the car radio with such force my nail cracked.

"Charlotte, your defining characteristic is your Achilles's Heel," said Ann. She was my best friend and business advisor for my marketing and PR firm.

Her words rang in my head from the previous day's conversation. "You are too nice and too trusting. While it makes you sweet and social and likeable, you have to learn not to trust people so quickly. I love that you seek the good in people, but not all people are good. Not all people deserve trust. Hackers are rampant and terrifying enough, but you just handed your phone to a serial cyber stalker. Forget your Southern girl training. This is the real world out there. Look over your shoulder. Keep your doors locked. Keep your purse zipped. And for God's sake, don't loan your phone to anyone else!"

When we travel together, people think she is my sister. Ann is my soul sister. We have a similar all-American classic look, but in my estimation, the camera loves her more. She works at it. She has no cellulite at all. She has hair extensions in her strawberry blonde loose curls, permanent makeup on her lips and eyelids, and veneers on her teeth. She had modeled in her twenties and still did some acting for fun. She has a successful career now, so she plays less, but she's still tons of fun. She's one of those people who is naturally beautiful on the inside and outside.

I am the consummate behind-the-scenes person. I like to write what the on-camera people, like Ann, say. I like to create emotions, and also sales for my clients, through the media. My relaxed, long effortless tresses are partly for Florida-girl casual looks but mostly for low maintenance. Loose ponytails generally outline my face, which was most often buried in a computer keyboard or book. I am a self-admitted content work-a-holic. Ann and I together had a long history of both working and playing together.

This morning, the fog inside my head fell into folders too many to list in the one hour ride to the private airport. Bad situations fueled an intense summer so far. Now with squalls dumping 20 fishermen in the ocean, hurricane season looms, as I am packed for an adventure at sea. The very early morning TV news announced two horrifying events: the capsized boat, and the Fox News Twitter hacker who tweeted that the President had been killed. He had not. The hoax was one in a mound of cyber warfare on an international scale. On an individual basis, the scare in my home had spooked me to my core.

This week I'll leave my own Casper the Ghost in my computers at home. At the last minute, I packed a two-pound MacBook Air; the temptation to write is most typically a blessing and a treat, but at the moment a curse and a heavy burden given the hellish nightmare I've endured.

This week will be escapism at it's best, an extreme digital detox. A one-hour flight to the islands will envelop me with a character building marlin fishing excursion. Man against the sea's largest fish consumes your body and mind with the marine activities, as it must for safety. On the drive to the airport, I visualized instead of a trolling sport fishing boat, running away in a performance boat with triple engines roaring and the hull planing to a faraway shore. But where am I to go? Can I in reality run away from that which is chasing me? Will I ever? The tight centrifugal force pulls me full circle back to the driver's seat of my 3 Series, without my attention, now driving entirely too fast, and trembling and shaking in a simmering fear for my own safety and concern for an inevitable global nightmarish doom.

I was startled back into the moment with a car tailgating me. It was a Volusia County police car with no police lights on. I pulled over to the side of the road and he followed me and parked behind me on the otherwise empty expanse.

"Can you tell me why you were going 130 miles-per-hour?" asked the stern African American policeman peering into my passenger window, which I had put down for him.

He seemed more concerned than disciplinary.

I was trying to switch gears but was still in such deep thought. I was trying hard to focus on what he was asking me.

"If you don't have a reason, I'm going to have to write you a $350 ticket. I followed you for five miles and you didn't even notice me. Are you OK?" the handsome face tilted to the side and leaned closer into the car. He looked young and innocent like he should be the community relations officer at an elementary school.

"No! I'm so sorry for speeding. I agree it's not safe and I'm not paying attention. You see, I'm starting to write this book about spirituality. All I can think about is cyber security and I'm really frightened. I've been hacked. I'm too engrossed in my thoughts and not paying attention to my life in general. This is just one more example of how all of this is adversely affecting me," I regretfully admitted and pointed to the thin manuscript, pads of paper and USB drive on the seat beside me.

I handed him my license and car registration and he retreated to his car. He came back a few minutes later with no ticket but a light lecture.

"I see you already have a ticket in the last month. If you don't pay attention, you will get more and lose your license. I'm not going to write your ticket today but promise me you will drive safely," he said and returned my papers.

I pulled back going east and he went west on State Road 44. I drove the speed limit.

The total eclipse of the sun by the new moon earlier in the week, shook every astrological sign with cosmic challenges, including my

Capricorn-grounded self. I read astrology updates that are e-mailed to me, and am astonished at the uncanny accuracy of my specific patterns and more global patterns of the universe. I have studied ancient traditional and non-traditional spiritual disciplines, and continue to ponder if they should all overlap somehow. It's possible. I personally believe there is a perfect order to the world, created by one God. I enjoy the research of all the teachings, and intelligent conversations that emerge in the circles of aware people.

The eclipse for my writing turned my world dark with a malicious, malevolent spirit, which invaded my life over the internet. The physical world dished up the fright factor, and my spiritual self confirmed the evil nature.

My life's destiny was to be a writer. I've always known what I was to be. In recent years, I prepared for my children's college years as my own time to get a quiet beach place to write, run my company remotely from a laptop, and travel the world experiencing coastlines and cultures. My destiny was to write and publish books, and produce films, exploring the human spirit to help heal the tender spots of humanity.

While the words flowed effortlessly as I worked on my all time pet project, my first novel, a dam kept building in the hard drive. The dam cramping the creative flow was software placed by a spirit of darkness within a man. Without the sun and light in my own spirit, no rainbows filled my pages. The pages went unwritten and empty. My head was filled with thoughts of self-survival. The engineers of apocalyptic destruction raped my words of peace and stole my sense of security.

When I arrived at the small private airport, I rushed into the lobby. I was 15 minutes late as I normally am. Punctuality isn't a gift of mine.

"Oh, hi," greeted the airline agent with a confused look, "We got your e-mail yesterday that you are moving your flight to August 30 and we processed your paperwork. What are you doing here today? Did I read it right?"

"You probably read something that was sent seeming as though it was sent from my e-mail, but that wasn't me. I've been hacked. I've been having terrible internet issues. A cyber stalker has infiltrated

4

my phone and computer and is ruining my life. I am here and I do want to board if you have a seat still," I pleaded with my shaking voice. I didn't want to go into all that explanation. I so had wanted to leave all that trouble behind for a week.

"Sure, there are only three people and a dog on this flight. We have your seat still. I'll cancel the August 30 flight. Let's get your baggage on. It's all good. We'll fix your travel plans," she comforted and came around the desk to help me board the six-seater plane preparing for take off.

That fishing trip was a year ago this week. Mental Post-it notes of paranoia are stuck with super glue to what should have been a post-card perfect week of fishing, in the middle of what up until then, had been an average to normal, to pleasant sort of life.

CHAPTER 2, DEJA VU FISHING TRIP A YEAR LATER

The drama escalated. The drama dropped to a background simmer. The drama ended. I thought it was over. It was not. Exactly a year later, after all I had endured and suffered to regain power over my life, fear invited himself back in my life. My iCalendar declared an impromptu Groundhog Day.

To reach the airport in New Smyrna Beach for a 7 a.m. flight, I had to awaken at 5 a.m. It seemed more efficient to simply stay awake. My house possessed the peacefulness of one thousand pins dropping to the metered metronome of the ceiling fan. The tinkling of the small metal wind chime, topped with a cross, hung on the wrought iron gate, and the clanking of the larger garden wind chimes added to the symphony of sounds. I hung the chimes as garden ornaments, but moreover as outside alarms if a person should enter my backyard at night. The soothing clacking and who-hooing of the train creschendoed into a thundering clatter as it made the 5 a.m. pass by my house as the alarm clock signaled the day had officially begun. The ADT security alarm had remained silent for the night. My physical being was safe. I relived the horrors of last summer in great detail in the darkened hours, hoping it was not re-entering my life this summer, exactly a year later.

Safety had been of great concern last summer for a few months, and gratefully ebbed to the background of life by last fall. As I prepared for this July's fishing trip near the end of this summer season in the Bahamas, the terror of a year past came crashing back into my life.

As I left last year for the islands, I was preparing to ship off all of my computers en masse to the computer guy to wipe them back to factory settings and re-install all of the software. I backed up important data, although for the most part, I made printed copies and re-created most of the files so I would not inadvertently re-install the technology terror. This July date, compared to the July date last year, had an eerily similar sense of pending doom.

I hadn't worked on my novels for a year. I wrote a novella with innocuous themes in the interim to get my writing fix. For this fishing trip, I'd planned to stay after on my writing sabbatical, with no internet, just long stretches of sugar sand beaches with crashing waves and my flowing words.

The novel would revolve around interesting characters from my Palm Beach and Bahamas adventures, revealing a light hearted how-to guide through the story line of how I experience spirituality. The novel in my head, yet to be committed to paper, except scraps piled in a box labeled "Rainbow Book," is pleasant and upbeat and focuses on promises. The main character, a writer, sees rainbows, and listens to God, Spirit, Intuition, Higher Power, Inner Guidance, whatever you call it. I call Him "V" for voice, which I experience through visions, hearing messages, and signals in the world, primarily lyrics of songs. I basically experience God through a "knowing" that will take a book, maybe books plural, to explain it all. In the current cultural panorama, with traditional religion and family values being slighted by a myriad of temporary replacements, spirituality didn't go anywhere. The spirit world is still alive, and active. Church memberships are suffering severe decline but spirituality is still with us patiently waiting to be listened to, to be heard. The working title is *Goldfish Die*, which requires a living soul to go beyond the fishbowl filled with narrow thinking or negative structured religious experiences, to experience spirituality in a larger, positive, transformative way. The goldfish has to jump in the ocean and let old-preconceived limiting notions die.

So, a year ago, I'm going about my life, riding around on my beach bike, taking breaks to sit on beaches with pen and paper, writing this novel about spirituality in the world. The dark side met my own light side with full force, showcasing the "opposite and equal reaction" theory. Basic Yen knocked my door down to get to Yang and kicked his butt.

The project got iced for months. Yesterday I took the USB flash drive named "Books Flowing" from the locked safety deposit box at the bank, and loaded the Adobe InDesign files onto the desktop of Mac Pro 2. This Mac has never been connected to the internet except at the Apple store when they updated the all new software they loaded for me. I bought it all brand new from the Apple store last summer. I've used it now for nearly a year successfully, and transferred files to the Mac Air via external drives if files required internet access.

I kept Mac Pro 1, with factory settings re-set, all new software, and have used it sparingly. I kept iMac and two iPhones and just unplugged them to keep for evidence should I need it for a criminal legal case. I bought a new iPhone, Mac Air and Mac Pro 2, which have fueled the business once I got it going again last fall after the lull of the summer meltdown.

So, I loaded my rainbow novel outline yesterday in preparation to edit the notes and write the delayed book on this trip. Within 30 seconds, the Mac Air which doesn't even have InDesign software on it, on the table two feet to my left, wiped my ocean wave screensaver, and burst to life scrolling left to right a dictionary word-of-the-day message on the monitor. The message read, "ef.fi.ca.cious Adjective: Successful in producing a desired or intended result; effective. Synonyms: effective – effectual – efficient – operative – potent."

"Oh! No!" I screamed at the top of my lungs as I lunged at the mini-monitor on the Mac Air and clicked the control, shift, 3 keys to take a screen shot and saved it to the desktop.

The screen saver waited a few seconds, which lingered for a seemingly hour-long breath or two, then wiped itself back to my ocean wave photo screensaver.

"Nooooooo! He's back," I whimpered to myself, "The zombie had slept for nearly a year. But who is back? And why? Is this a real cyber stalker or supernatural communicator? Why me?"

CHAPTER 3, DAMNED?

A year ago, I wouldn't have paid any attention to technology issues on the news. In the last year, I had become acutely aware that infringements upon privacy and threats to safety that were being reported more and more, including the ones today.

Today on the pre-dawn news, the anchor read the headline news, "The online dating website EHarmony was hacked yesterday and 10,000 usernames and passwords to personal profiles were posted online. EHarmony advised users to change their passwords immediately and is looking into the security breach. They join Yahoo, LinkedIn, Gmail, Hotmail and AOL as targets for hackers. This week only 505,000 users were breached, and with over 300 million active e-mail users in Yahoo alone, this represents less than 1 percent of internet users."

"Really? Those affected don't think the word 'only' applies. Their lives could be in total disorder. How about not E-harmony but disharmony? Nothing in e-world is harmonious," I yelled at the TV, "Is anything sacred or safe?"

The news continued, "While the federal government strives to pass cyber security legislation, citizens are concerned about an intrusive federal role in basic communications rights and excessive burdens on businesses. Instead of Homeland Security, the Senate now is considering a public-private partnership for establishing standards for critical infrastructure. A government spokesperson said the danger of a massive cyber attack is clear and present."

"Neither choice is good. We are damned if we do and damned if we don't. We have to protect ourselves online but we don't want government regulating communication. These cyber criminals are causing the digital damnation of civilized society. We are being forced to prioritize between our first amendment right to free speech and our global safety and security. Both are paramount. We need both, not either. We don't want the government regulating our cyber conversations. We don't want to have to fund the manpower it would take to regulate everyday online communication. Just visualize an airport with all the red tape, and now shove all that mandate into a chip and this is now your internet access line. Now picture standing in that line at the airport and all your conversations have to be monitored by TSA. The flights would never leave ground. All the automation of the internet could be muted and snail mail reestablished. Or worse. Ban internet communications? What could be a solution?" I wondered to myself.

I hopped in my car, heading for the New Smyrna Beach airport in a deja vu chilling hour long drive recalling exactly a year ago.

I heard the ding of a text message during the drive, and pulled over in case it was from my fishing buddies, Owen or Ed his boat captain. Owen is my all-time favorite client for my Public Relations firm. He has blue eyes the color of the sky and silver hair, cut weekly. His nails are always manicured. His clothes are always pressed. He looks like he walked right out of Neiman Marcus catalog, always put together. He is a medium sized physically fit man, all man, and strong in every way. He speaks perfect English with a vast vocabulary. He actually speaks five languages fluently. I have the utmost respect for his business dealings, which I whole-heartedly support him with marketing and public relations services over six continents. He has an uncanny, innate ability to create win-win solutions between the business world, governments, natural resources, and communities. With every corporate take-over or sale, there is always a compassionate, thorough, thoughtful conversation about the people who are part of the company and the community around the company. Owen is a people person. He is a self-made wealthy, powerful man, but first-and-foremost, he is a good man. He is down-to-earth and just as comfortable, maybe more so, in fishing tournament T-shirts and khaki shorts as he is in $5,000 business suits. Whether we are building marketing plans for his businesses or hunting for fish, Owen is perfect polite company, with the most intelligent, fascinating stories of his life's work and world travels. As much time as I spend with him, I still learn something new and interesting every time I am with him. He makes me think. I am proud to be a part of his success. His success allowed me to be successful. Without him, I would not have a PR firm.

Owen and Captain Ed would sometimes ask me to bring provisions to the boat from Florida where shopping was more abundant and less expensive. It wasn't either of my travel mates. It was evil calling again. The text on the iPhone read, from 251-84, "Guess What?

The word assassination was invented by William Shakespeare. For help call 188889."

So, maybe this was random spam or maybe it threaded to other words to be sent for a complete message. I wouldn't have thought as much of it had it not been paired with the screen saver message, the word "efficacious." The cyber terror of last summer started with screen saver words. So, now this message was really creeping me out as I strung it together in my head, "effective assassination" and William Shakespeare, the writer of tragedies. It was on this same rural 20-minute stretch of State Road 44 that started last July's digital detox and my plan to take back control of my life. After a long, diligent struggle, I had successfully regained my life, until yesterday.

I was nervously twisting on my finger my long string of pearls around my neck, almost choking myself before I was conscious of my action. Not only were robbers on the internet, but also still on the streets. With the sluggish economy, there had been an increase in home burglaries in affluent areas where the robbers empty a house closet by closet, drawer by drawer, and leave in short order with cash, jewelry, and electronics. I tenaciously keep the burglar alarm on at my home, but with extra precaution this week, I took all the valuables that would fit into the safety deposit box to the bank. I had to gather them from what I thought were brilliant hiding places in emptied soap boxes or cereal boxes, squirreled all over my home. If they got one, surely another would be left. Ann told me those all get emptied onto your floor when the robbers hit a home. This summer, I let my college age daughter sift through all the jewelry given to me from her dad and from my parents. I'd prefer for her to lose it than someone take it from me. I made an appointment with a jewelry broker to trade in what was left for serious bling to wear every day, to enjoy and to touch. My compulsive obsession over my bling I decided was because it was tangible, so I could see it and hold it and protect it in a very different manner than my technical treasures. Feeling safe and empowered again would be a process, a long process, with two steps forward, three back.

I read a stack of fashion magazines on the one-hour plane trip to the Bahamas to keep stimulated on words like "pretty" and "positive." Orange swimsuits are in. Wear sunscreen. The fashion capital is New York and Paris. Easy concepts. I brought my favorites *Vanity Fair* and *Garden and Gun*. I could see the words but I couldn't concentrate enough to comprehend what I was reading. My mind was fully occupied with the mystery before me. The total lack of sleep didn't help either.

A cursory customs check at Marsh Harbour airport, and I was on the five-minute cab ride. The van was unusually sparkling clean and neat. Taxis or cabs in the islands can be almost any vehicle that runs. The cheerful woman had the typical Bahamian cab driver Bible tucked beside her water bottle in the front seat. She was humming to the Gospel station on the radio. She had photos of her family taped to the front dash. She sported a bright flowered dress around her round body with red strappy-heeled sandals. She wore the bright make-up some of the island women do with teal blue eye shadow painted all the way up to her eyebrow and bright pink lipstick thick and layered with lip gloss. Her hair was laid straight and flipped up into a curl around her head in a '50s do. She was chatty about how proud she was of her daughter. I wondered if that daughter was at home right now on the internet like many teens of the world; we're all connected in the cloud servers. When we came to the potholes full of water from rain, she slowed down to a stop as to not splash mud on the fresh wash of the gray Chrysler.

"I need a part for the axle. It's $400 and I can't afford it yet. She rides great but I have to be careful in the bumps till I get her fixed," the taxi driver reported.

She dropped me off at the marina office and helped me unload my luggage. I gave her $100 for the $27 fare and a tip to go towards the broken part. If anyone understood about the liability of unseen brokenness, it was I. Her broken part could be fixed. I'd have to work more on my inner brokenness. She gave me a big, warm, Bahama mama hug. The Bahamians are still fully engaged in the physical life. A computer can't replace a hug, a smile, or a handshake to communicate camaraderie or gratitude.

CHAPTER 4, IS THE HONOR BAR LOST?

On this seventh trip to the islands of the summer, I headed directly to the boat. The positive ions of the salt air and the vitamin D of the morning sun worked on my body while the serene stroll along the marina soothed my spirit. The past evening's storm showered the shore with a sparkling fresh wash. Everything glistened including me from the hint of perspiration in the 90-degree early morning walk. The meaty curly tail lizards dashed from under showered hibiscus bushes and tropical plants, and the seagulls dove for fish. Under the water around the docks, big circles of smaller fish jumped for life as predators below corralled their breakfasts. Boatloads of eager fishermen were carrying ice to their coolers, buying their live bait, and talking over coffee about the day's perfect flat sea, with up to 5 knot wind. The flags were still.

Captain Ed passed me on the dock with his pre-boat-launch fifth-gear get-her-done work-mode demeanor. He had a preppy businessman look to him if you toned down the tan and suited him. He was 50-ish with a big toothy smile, brown hair with gray flecks worn a little longer than clean cut and generally tucked under a ball cap. He was six-three like my son, with a Tarzan physique. He had intense brown eyes with crow's feet and wrinkles on his forehead when he concentrated.

Captain Ed was carrying Diet Cokes and Chelsea's Best waters. We joked sometimes about the bottled water in the islands being tap water bottled. You never really knew for sure if bottled water was safer than tap water.

"Bahamian's best water I see," I said.

Captain wasn't in a joking mood. He asked in his loud raspy voice, "So, the boat broker in Miami said this one's already up for sale again. We haven't even gotten her wet yet. I just got her spit shined and pretty and loaded up all the gear. It took an hour just to get on all the snorkel gear he just bought. Owen's taking crazy pills. What in the hell is going on?"

"We'll all find out shortly. He's been giving me cryptic messages, too. He didn't mention the boat, but I know my PR projects might be abruptly ending along with the fees, which I'm not excited about," I shrugged.

13

Owen then rang the iPhone for me to meet him in the office of the Boat Harbor Marina. Owen and I and Captain Ed were taking the virgin voyage of his new sport fishing 65-foot Hatteras named Blue Daze. He had been watching it on the webcam at the marina and today we'd actually take her out. Captain had moved over $46,000 worth of fishing equipment, and stocked it with food, provisions and $4,000 in diesel fuel.

"Let's leave the technology here in the marina office. I had Captain leave his already. Phones, computers all need to stay here. We're going to have a fishing adventure the old-fashioned way with boat, man and beast," Owen directed.

I pulled my iPhone and the Mac Air from my pink pirate backpack and he dropped his three-year-old Razor flip phone and IBM laptop in the marina's back office for storage during our fishing trip. IBM had been one of Owen's consulting clients. He was a loyal guy. He had an Ivy league education through scholarships and Old-School real world education in international leadership. He was my client and in code-talk I knew this was as much of a business trip as it was a fun fishing trip.

"I have an update for you about my computer security issues. They appear to be resurfacing as of yesterday, so I'm happy to leave my technology here for a few days," I told Owen, the boat owner and my biggest client.

"I know how scared you were last year. I have my own security issues, which I'll tell you about on the boat, offshore, away from all electronics. I have people listening now. I'll need you to do exactly as I say for the next few days and keep Captain in line with my directives," said Owen as we walked down the dock.

Captain already had the boat warmed and ready. We pulled the lines from the dock and headed south along Great Abaco Island towards our destination of Freeport. We planned for an eight-hour fishing expedition for the day on the mirror calm waters with 5 knot light breeze.

Owen started our trip with his gregarious tour-guide mode. Even if you had been with him before in the same area, he would give an automatic account of the location and history of an area. He boated so often with so many people over so many years, he probably really didn't remember you had been with him five times already out of a certain marina. I liked hearing it even for the fifth time.

"We have to use caution over these reefs with only 10-feet of water and 6-feet under the boat," he pointed out as he steered the vessel towards deeper safer water. He turned south after the water washed from teal to turquoise to royal blue.

"On the right is the underwater national park. See the moorings where boats can hook up to and people can dive and snorkel? It's a world wonder," he said.

Five minutes later he added, "Next on Great Abaco is Little Harbor and Pete's Pub. It used to be an honor bar where you would pour your own drink and leave cash. Now it's next to Winding Bay, which is a Ritz Carlton resort. I don't associate the islands with golf, but I'm not one to sit on one island either. Pete's Pub is a tourist attraction now, which probably helps him sell his sculptures. He's got a foundry and an art museum there."

He paused, he then added, "The honor bar is gone. Honor is indeed gone."

The three of us sat in the fly bridge as Owen steered his new toy and steered the conversation, what little there was so far, "Up here on the right, you see the light house at Hole-In-The-Wall at the southern tip of Great Abaco Island. If you look at the huge rock formation at the tip, you see the big round hole. Some things are just simple and direct. Some things make sense."

"So Charlotte, how many fish are we going to boat today?" Owen asked.

I thought for a minute, had a vision of six whales, and responded, "Six."

"Six it is," Owen confirmed.

It was our "how many" game. He asked my prediction each fishing trip, and would be amused at dinner when we'd recap the day to find I had an uncanny statistical accuracy for predicting fish. He would periodically ask me about various topics, and I'd sometimes have to have him clarify, "What do I think, or what do I know?" The answers might be different. What I think would be based on my thoughts, and what I know would be based on spiritual input and interpretation.

CHAPTER 5, DEEP TROUBLE IN DEEP WATER

Owen motioned for Captain to steer and for me to go down to the cockpit.

We sat on the cockpit bench for a few minutes admiring the picture perfect flat fishing day now with no wind, no chop, no swell.

"So, it's worse than I thought when I updated you Tuesday. We have a real PR problem on our hands, yes, but we have a significant problem that PR can't fix. A real problem," said Owen. Then he took in and let out a deep breath and stood silent for a moment.

"I've thought of everything. I've researched an offshore tech army of Russians, Chinese and Indians. To strike back against the enemy might make matters worse. They know my every move, and those of everyone around me. As I told you, the Mexicans will not honor the pending $120 million contract for the oil company sale. They say since our rigs are spewing oil into the Gulf, that it's worth only $20 million. You know I need the cash to save my other 20 companies, which are all gasping for cash infusions. The oil company was the salvation for all of the companies, all of the people in all of those companies, and for my retirement," Owen pursed his lips and took a break. We sat silently.

"Operating like a drug cartel, the Mexican company is dishonest and destructive. Even their officers are a fraud. Mexico is home to international companies, including this one with Mexicans listed as the officers. I've researched who is actually behind this terror, and some are Mexicans but not all. Their greed and malicious control is now bathing my beloved Gulf coast fish and birds in the thick goo of the grim reaper. The Gulf was just recovering from the last blow. After college, my first career was in the oil industry based out of New Orleans. They have hit me in my soft spot. I love the place," sighed Owen.

I had never seen this stellar man in this weakened state with any PR issue, or any issue at all. We had overcome hostile corporate takeover attempts more than once. We had navigated legal investigations of some of his top executives. We had dealt with media badgering when his son committed suicide. I've seen this man in battle. I had never seen this man like this.

He continued, "The Mexican company is forcing my hand to sell

16

for the reduced price by Monday. They have the cash to stop the oil spill and keep the operations going. They created the oil spill when their malware cyber-sabotaged the drill, forcing it faster and harder until it spun out of control and cracked under the pressure. The rig guys could watch it spinning out of control but couldn't stop it. The Mexicans claim it wasn't them, of course, but my sources confirm it was. After Monday, they threatened a cyber attack of all of my companies, one per week, until I transfer the oil company for the reduced price."

He took a pregnant pause and glanced at me. I sat motionless and offered nothing. I had no solution or even any words of comfort, which was unusual for me.

"Without the full price, the other companies will fail anyway due to lack of funding. If I tried all that I could as an honest business-person, to save my companies and they failed, I could live with myself. To sell out, knowing the Mexicans will likely destroy the oil companies anyway, gives me an out, but leaves all that I love in peril still. Am I to sell my companies, and by that I mean thousands of individual faces, people, to an uncertain fate? It can all be avoided with an honest deal. Can I stop the destruction? Will I be forced to watch the demise of all that my life has cherished and nurtured un-der the heavy hand of bribery, blackmail and criminal activity? This hell threatens us all. I am just one victim. There are multitudes of horror stories yet to come. I'm not sure we can stop it but I'm going to try with every resource I have. My oil companies are just the first. They plan to control every U.S. oil operation down to every pump at every gas station," he grieved.

He was sketching with pen on paper as he did in deep thought. He had circles representing all his companies, with lines representing all the people, he added a globe and drew a big circle around the whole illustration. He ripped the paper from the pad, wadded it up, and tossed it like a baseball at Yankee stadium into the center of the eight-foot-tall rooster tail waterspout behind the boat.

"Paper is biodegradable. Almost anything left in saltwater long enough will disappear in fact," he said.

"Nothing is forever," he added in a whisper.

"So, when was the last time you took your kids camping to learn

17

survival skills?" he asked.

"When they were little," I responded puzzled by his shift of topic.

"It's important for families to have a survival plan just in case a tragedy happens. You live in Florida so think about preparing for a hurricane. Have gas in your car. Have plenty of fresh bottled water, non-perishable food, candles, batteries and flashlights and such. Designate a place to meet if tragedy ever does occur. Call your kids when we get to land and remind them of your family plan. Tell them to always keep survival items on hand. Why wait and shop when an emergency strikes? Emergencies, by their very nature, don't always send warning signs," he said.

This was not the normal Owen father figure extraordinaire that I knew. This man was foreboding and somber. He didn't have his weekly-haircut clean look and the silver tufts flew straight up. His blue eyes looked neon against the bloodshot red background. He slumped a bit instead of his normal militant-erect stance, and he looked gaunt like he had missed some meals. I didn't know how to respond to this Ominous Owen, so I didn't. I sat silently.

He had the proverbial bigger fish to fry, so I didn't share with him the details of my own second wave of cyber scare. We were both victims. He had coached me through my hacker last summer and now was my turn to support him. This terror threads through the meek and mighty, and as terrified as I was for myself and still am for myself, Owen's problem is also my problem. He is my client; I'll lose that income. If the oil companies get destroyed, the whole country is in serious trouble. I thought maybe I should tell him about my two incidents in case my message was intended for him, not for me. Captain's voice shook me from my deep concentration back to fishing.

"Frigate birds two-o'clock," Captain yelled from the fly bridge and gave a sharp turn towards the offshore birds hunting for baitfish being corralled up by feeding dolphin and tuna. Captain and Owen were the supreme hunters of the sea. They, with variations of their fishing teams, won tournament after tournament for billfish and off-shore fish, and always marlin. Owen had caught every type of marlin including blue, white, black and striped.

Mid-morning found us over the Canyon, an underwater ledge created by the Antilles Current, which housed big fish. The tackle was ready with cedar plugs for tuna and colorful lures. Owen and Captain dropped the outriggers and four lines splashed out from 100-feet to 300-feet behind the trolling vessel. Captain swung through the thick bird feeding spot three times then the lines squealed.

Owen pulled in the first fish, a skipjack. Captain released the hook and threw the fish back into the ocean. He cleaned off weeds caught on two of the lines, released them back and we continued to troll. If weeds are caught in the lures, Captain can see it better from 20-feet higher than us at sea level. A higher perspective helps you see obstacles and opportunities.

"Those fish look like tuna but skip across the top of the water like a silver bullet. You can't eat jacks. Those bullets shoot a hole in our clocks is what they do. They have us chasing them all over hell's half acre and wasting our time," complained Captain as he stomped back up the stairs.

Within ten minutes, Owen pulled in a 25-pound yellow fin tuna and I boated a 20-pounder. Captain pulled the hooks from the fish, sliced them under their gills to bleed them, then put the lines back out and he was back up top, heading back to the birds. Three lines hit and we all pulled in tuna, five in all, about 100 pounds of fish.

"In Florida, fresh tuna is $18 per pound, so we just iced $1,800 in fish. I've got three charters lined up because the guys know I can fill coolers with fish," Captain beamed and went back to run the boat. He was uncertain of his own fate and was starting in on the job-security lines.

I watched the life flee from the gasping fish left to bleed in the blood bath on the back corner of the boat. I preferred to have the fish put in coolers so we don't have to witness this segment of the fishing experience. Today, why not watch? The tuna going about their tuna-day, hooked, yanked, stabbed and left gasping with imminent death were not unlike the corporations we were discussing, every bit as much surprised, stunned, shocked and just plain screwed.

"I don't like to watch them die. I remember my first dolphin that I caught. I kept checking on him in the cooler. In his eye, I could see him pleading for me to release him back to the sea," I said.

"Fish all die. If they weren't your dinner on the boat, they would be dinner today, or another day under the sea. Don't feel badly.

Every fish is food," said Owen.

Owen was always so logical and could shine a positive spin on any business situation. He had the Midas Touch. I still wasn't so sure the cannibalized fish agreed their death was positive.

"The birds disappear in the open sea as quickly as they appear, like ghosts," I noted as we turned our heads in every direction looking for the frigate flock.

"It's like each of us has a malicious ghost hiding in our closets, under our beds, in our car trunks and in our desks at our offices. It's terrifying but you can't get rid of them because you can't even prove they are there. At least with a ghost, you could have an exorcism or séance or something to drive the guy out. With these electronic ghosts, you can move to a new house, trade cars, get a new office, trade in all your phones and computers, but the ghosts just follow you there; and you might just inherit someone else's bad ghosts," I analyzed. My analogy didn't comfort Owen. He acted like he didn't hear it and continued with his own line of thinking.

"The tactics they are using on me, powered by misinformation and fueled by greed, will spread like wildfire to every faction of society from our own backyards. We've invited them in with our lack of stringent, diligent safeguards. It's like we left the gate open to our backyard and a wild Rottweiler family moved in and now if you don't feed them daily, they'll break through your sliding glass door and let themselves into your kitchen for a ham sandwich. They know no boundaries. They have no rules, no souls," he continued.

He took a break and picked up the five tuna, now totally lifeless, and put them in the 50-gallon white marine cooler full of ice. He loosened the hose and rinsed the blood through the drain holes.

Particularly in the context of the conversation, it was a relief to have the image of death put aside.

"We signed the oil deal last month on the DeBait II before I sold my partnership interest in that boat. The Mexicans know that out of all of my companies, Blue Water, LLC, the boat charter company, is my heart and soul and where I was headed with my life after I sold the oil company. They'll hit this boat Monday as the next target to get to me. They will forego the more prominent national and international targets to get me to personally crumble. I've given this a great deal of thought," Owen said.

All I could think was, "I am a minnow in the corporate sea with my little PR firm on one little reef. Owen represents the international pelagic mighty marlin of the sea. Owen is directly and indirectly responsible for a multitude of little minnows, and medium sized fish, and other marlins, too! We all benefit from a capitalistic leader-driven economy and civilized society. Hackers are hacking at us, our leaders, our lifestyles and our very lives. I'm going to do all I can to help him capture and kill the digital enemy, both my spy and this corporate espionage criminal."

"So, what are you going to do?" I sighed.

I turned from watching for tuna birds into the eyes of my long time client, mentor and best friend, and from below his Costa Del Mar sunglasses, I could see the blue eyes dripping the sadness of defeat down his cheek. The marlin was crying.

He didn't have a PR problem. This former Navy Seal and CIA operative had a major international crisis problem. I couldn't help. What would I do? I felt numbness climb up my body like an ana-conda and choke me until I burst into tears. I held my breath so I'd stop and wiped my tears with my beach towel.

"They plan to drive up oil prices. Once my oil deal closes, they plan to close on the other eight largest U.S. oil rig companies under contract. Then they have cyber attacks planned to digitally destroy and burn up all the power plants in the U.S. within 60 days. They have a bug to shut down the cooling systems. They are small-minded. They don't understand the impact of their feeble but fatal plan. They think they will sell more oil if the power plants are out of order. It's not logical. They saw my e-mail address access that file that outlines their sordid plan. They notified me that if I alert the President, the military, the media, anyone, they will accelerate their plan of digital destruction. I fell into the plan by accident while I was securing my personal, private files from the mainframe of the oil company. I never should have co-mingled my personal and my business life on that computer but it started decades ago. That is just where I kept my financial records. Before there were personal com-puters, there were behemoth-sized giants that filled entire rooms. My assistant had my files there, and they stayed there until now. That is all beside the point. The point is we are all in imminent global danger," he said.

We sat quiet for what seemed like an hour. I didn't move. I didn't know how to respond.

"There is more," he broke the silence.

"More?" I gasped.

"You know how Rick put spyware on your devices, then it opened Pandora's Box for Sick waiting quietly in the shadows to wreak havoc on your cyber world, pointing blame at the chaos that Rick created? Well, the Mexican company is my Rick and a huge national security issue is looming that is my Sick. It's like we're trying to stop a cat burglar, and Hitler is standing behind him just waiting for him to pick the lock so he can goosestep right on in," he said.

"The very innovation that defines us as Americans will destroy us if we do not take immediate action. Not just us as the world leader, but chaos will ripple through the world, which is teetering at the tip of a cliff of peril. Not just my own oil company, but global companies daily are fighting and protecting against cyber attacks with a vengeance. You don't hear about it because it's classified information. An information leak would create a self-imploding crash of civilized behavior. A civil war would likely start. I've participated with the Secret Service on twelve teams with significant missions so far to overt attacks. What we learned is the ominous entity in the background has collaboration and corruption at top levels on American soil. When the Mexican company strikes against the oil companies, the entity I'll call "Nine" will at an instant, shut down all the cellular towers, internet services and broadcast media. Communication stops. Nobody can communicate except for this vicious group who has developed their own unique communication devices. Nine-eleven will pale in comparison. They will implement "Nine" followed by their plan of "Eleven." I'm shaking in my Dockers, and it takes a lot to scare me," Owen explained.

I highly suspected Owen was a CIA agent but this was the first time he admitted Secret Service activities.

All I could think of is, "Why is this marlin here fishing with me right now? Shouldn't he be with his CIA buddies in a mega-power pow-wow somewhere solving this apocalyptic threat?"

CHAPTER 6, FISHING FOR SOLUTIONS TO PORT LUCAYA

"Whales," yelled Captain.

Off to the right, I pulled the Nikon out, zoomed to huge black ovals in the navy sea, and clicked eight whales in one shot. I raced to the other side and counted 15 whales splashing as their blowholes atomized water. I snapped a photo and only caught three up, but one with his tail high in the air.

"So, 23 whales, some 50-feet long, must be a positive sign. You don't see whales every trip," I tried to add a positive note as I checked the shots in my camera.

Captain slowed the boat, and put it in automatic drive to come to the cockpit. Below the boat emerged a half dozen playful dolphins, the porpoise kind not the mahi-mahi we fish for. Dolphins cheer you up with their childlike playfulness. They said their hellos, bobbing up and down, and prancing in the air with high jumps, and followed the whales off into the blue expanse.

Captain had us at Gingerbread now and was gearing up for bottom fishing. He changed out the rods for two smaller ones geared with weights and three hooks per line with fish meat and attached to batteries to power the reels to pull the fish up quickly.

I took the break in the action to go inside to the boat's kitchen and get our box lunches. It was 1 p.m. now and the sun was directly overhead beating down on us. I had forgotten to wear my hat and I could feel the singe of the sun upon the fragile skin on my face. I grabbed the straw cowboy hat with the shell adornments I had bought at the "Staw Market" in Harbor Island last trip. I've always loved the islands and the charm. Such misspellings on the signs and the random variations to structured life enchanted me. On the islands, remembering to be happy took priority over remembering to put an "r" on a sign. Recalling the hat purchase made me smile. I lowered my ponytail so the hat would fit and joined the men outside.

Captain cheered, "We're gonna' drop some bombs. I can see schools all over the radar."

He continued with his chatter, unaware of our somber tone, "There's Bimini right there where the islanders rioted against the police when they shot a suspect. The rioters sunk the police cars

and burned down the police station a few years back. It's the closest island to Florida, in Ft. Lauderdale, so it's a shame the islanders
reacted like that. I hear the tourism is coming back. Speaking of
tourism, on the left there on Great Isaac, see the big cruise ships
docked there out of Cape Canaveral and Palm Beach?"

"It's always an interesting look at human behavior, how one person, or one small group can change the course of history of an
entire group of people, for better or for worse. In these Bahamas
islands, where you can travel to several in one day even, you can see
such distinct differences and nuances of each island culture," I added as I looked around and wondered if either of those two islands
might be suitable to escape to if the U.S. imploded. I also pondered
that the three cruise ships docked at the island were full of potential
trapped victims if a tech-hacker bad guy targeted their internet. My
mind thought up tragedies as never before.

Captain watched the electronics from the fly bridge and screamed,
"now." Owen and I released our lines for bottom fishing. It would
take several minutes for the lines to sink 500 feet. We each attached
the base of the rods into the cup of the fishing belts and gently lifted
the lures emulating how a fish might swim along the bottom of the
ocean until we felt bites. We each got nibbles at the same time and
pushed the buttons on the reels with our right thumbs as our left
hands held the reels and guided the line on the reels with our left
thumbs so as not to create "nests" in the reels.

"I have that spider wire thick on the reel so it takes less time to
pull up the fish, but it's easier to get a nest and you see it would get
stuck so pay attention to keeping the lines flat on the reel," Captain
advised as he bent over the back of the boat to grab the leader line,
"Nice strawberry groupers. Put the lines back. The fish are waiting
to commit suicide down there. They are thick green on the radar."

We repeated the process several times pulling up four more strawberry groupers, two black groupers of a larger size and red snapper.
Captain put them in the cooler as he brought them in the boat. He
always took the fish off the hooks. We reel. He unhooks the fish. He
reloads fresh fish for bait on the hooks. Teamwork.

"The fish world is brutal. We are putting pieces of a dead fish on
a hook so his sealife neighbor fish will eat him. And his fish friend

does eat him. Works every time. Each fish is looking right and left, up and down, all day and all night because someone bigger than him wants to eat him alive for lunch. That's pretty gross actually. The fish get eaten by one of their own totally alive. Yuck," I commented, shaking my head. I was concentrating too much on the fish deaths thought the men. They didn't comment.

We fished the spot until the fish stopped biting, and Captain changed out the gear again.

"Let's find some birds and troll a little more on the way into Port Lucaya," said Captain from above.

"We're thick in the Devil's Triangle. These are Hemmingway's waters where he invented sport fishing. He's still the big fish around here," said Owen back in his tour-guide mode and at least seeming as though he was focused on the fishing.

Ten minutes into the motoring, we all saw it at the same time, a giant tuna bubble in the water the size of a small carousel with birds flying in a perfect circle overhead diving for and picking up bait fish. Below would be dolphin, tuna and / or wahoo surrounding the school of smaller fish, making a living bubble net.

I snapped incredibly detailed photos with my zoom that could have made a spread in *Marlin* magazine. I admired my photography trophy for a moment and tucked away the camera in the backpack and got ready for action.

At my request, Owen took the left side and I the right. "I prefer the starboard side so I sit and reel inside the boat. On the port side, you are hanging over the edge of the boat to reel with your right hand. It makes me feel vulnerable because I know mammoth marlin, sharks and stingrays might jump up and take me out just for fun. Remember that story of the woman in the Keys who was just standing there on a boat and an eight-foot stingray flew up and landed on her flopping all over the boat? It happens," I reminded him of my preference.

A reel screamed. Owen got it. Another screamed and I got it. Sometimes I leave the heavy offshore rods in the holders on the side of the boat, and sometimes I lift them. I lifted it and started to reel. He was putting up a vigorous fight then totally gave into my dominance.

25

I could hear Captain yelling from above, "It's not a gun. Don't point it at the fish! Point up the rod and keep the drag on the fish. No slack! Where is your head?"

I snapped to and realized Captain was talking to me. Fishing is like swimming after a while. It's automatic. I was so distracted by the conversation with Owen, my "automatic" needed mental manual manipulation. The lack of drag gave the fish freedom to shake loose from the hook and he made his way to freedom. I reeled in the line quickly to get it out of the way of Owen's live line and grabbed another line being pulled by a meaty challenger.

Five minutes of reeling, and Owen brought in the first dolphin or mahi-mahi of the day, a 30-pounder. I pulled up a yellow fin tuna, and another, and another, and another, eight total between us. Owen pulled up a wahoo, too. In 20 minutes time, we raised a whole cooler of fish. Then it went flat. Just like that. Fish flopping all over the cockpit gasping for air, then no fish bites at all. Poof. Gone.

"Fish get smart. After eight tuna get yanked from the water, they realize, 'hey, where's everyone going?' and they get smart and leave. Fish get smart and you have to move on to a new spot. Fishing is all about moving. Fish don't keep still and neither can we," Captain was gleefully chatting as he corralled the flopping fish and as we reeled in the lines for the day.

I noticed we didn't target marlin at all. We always targeted marlin. Owen didn't even talk to Captain about what we'd fish for. Captain had his own agenda it seemed to bring in fish. It must have been survival instinct to stock up on fish for food if the boat was going to be sold. Also, fish is informal island currency. Captains have a sixth sense about the weather, tides and fishing conditions, and probably more so about their owners.

As we headed towards Port Lucaya, I said, "I'm counting happy hour in dog beers tonight. I could use an island style rum drink. Owen, you up for a yellow bird?"

I got a thumbs-up from Owen, and went inside to mix some cocktails for the ride in.

"Five o'clock somewhere is heading for seven, not that time matters in the Bahamas," I pointed out as we pulled into the marina. It had been a long journey and our longest fishing day ever. I wondered why we went such a long distance when all the year-end parties were gearing up in the Abacos. I didn't ask. Not much made sense about now. I was literally along for the ride.

I checked into my room, had a quick shower. I met Owen at an outside table at Agave, my favorite Latin fusion restaurant in the brightly colored Colonial-style tin-roofed village of shops surrounding the Count Basie Marketplace square. The band was warming up on the stage to start the live music and dancing. Owen had given the chef a Baggie of our fresh tuna to prepare. Bahamians can cook fish.

"I saw the Irish pub closed. How did that happen in a sea of fishermen, sailors and tourists?" I asked. I had toasted green beer on more than one St. Patty's Day in Bahamian bars including that one.

"It's a season. This was a hot spot for the fishing tournaments. Five years ago, ten years ago, we'd have 100 boats and 500 anglers competing over a week of fishing, fun and male bonding. Last year, the tournament here had 15 boats. The guys compete to win money and with that small number of boats, the calcutta is so small, it won't even cover the fuel," said Owen.

Owen tapped a few drops from a bottle of Tabasco onto the center of the vinyl tablecloth. With the light wind, the flies were swarming looking for their own dinner. Flies don't like Tabasco as much as us Southerners do.

He ordered a bottle of fume blanc. I prefer Chardonnay but he didn't ask. I'd order California whites over French whites, but again, I wasn't asked. I didn't really care. I decided I'd order dessert, too. What wine doesn't cure, sugar cures.

The first bottle went down rather quickly. Owen was quiet, but not acting unusual given our conversation on the boat. He continued to talk about the state of fishing and boating for polite conversation.

"I got a great deal on this new boat. She had very little hours on her and virtually no wear and tear. She had been dry docked for a year. Some say it's bad to keep boats out of the water; they were designed to float, not to fight gravity in a hanger. The sport fishing models are being replaced by the go-fast boats. The theory is that with all the money you save in maintenance, you can stay in the hotels at the marinas. There's never enough sleeping space for all your

27

crew on a boat anyway, so you always get rooms. The money guys are getting the mega yachts as floating condos and taking the go-fast boats along to fish. Sure, it makes sense but I'm still a sporty guy. I really like this new boat," said Owen.

Captain joined us, missing the opportunity to ask questions about the boat topic in play.

A second bottle of wine was served with Captain's Kalik beer. We toasted a very productive fishing day.

"You know, right here in Freeport, just like in Nassau, it's been fished by the settlers for 200 years and overfished for over 50 years so it's hard to get a bite right around here. You have to go out further like we do in the tournaments to see fish," Captain commented.

"We saw fish today my friend. She was right, six. She's generally accurate, just not always exactly what you think. Exact is in a detail, in the interpretation. Not six fish but six species. We caught grouper, snapper, mahi-mahi, tuna and one wahoo. Lots of tuna today. And we threw back the skip jack. That's six. Plus we saw dolphins and whales. The sea was smooth and the fishing was superb. The sea was kind to us today," Owen recapped.

The chef prepared a colorful plate presentation of a fresh assortment of steamed vegetables fanning out from a seared fresh tuna steak in the center of each of our plates. We enjoyed our dinners and said our goodnights. Life was good in the moment. In the moment is all life really is anyway.

CHAPTER 7, CROSS CURRENTS TO BIMINI

We met at Zorba's in Port Lucaya for breakfast. The Bahamas culture comfortingly reminds me of the Deep South at times. The waitress called me "honey" and I ordered my favorite comfort food, grits, with breakfast.

We boarded Blue Daze and Captain pulled us up to the fuel dock to pour another $4,000 in fuel into the belly of the boat.

I had a plastic cup of Gatorade and in the morning sun, saw a rainbow in the reflection of the plastic. I was seeing rainbows everywhere a year ago. They were likely still around, I just hadn't noticed maybe. This was clearly a rainbow. I showed it to Owen to validate my sighting.

"Yes, it's a rainbow. You like rainbows. It's a good sign for you. Drink it up," said Owen.

"So missy, how many fish in the boat today?" he inquired.

I thought for a minute, saw two dolphin in my mind, and responded, "Two."

That seemed like a disappointing small number after yesterday's fish frenzy, but he accepted it with a nod. He looked at his fingers and counted, one, two fingers and stared back at the marina village.

"Sunday," he breathed out.

"I was talking two fish, not two days," I clarified, knowing the stakes were sky high in decisions this weekend. I didn't mind Owen tapping into my intuition but decisions about the safety of the world were not decisions I should have a voice in.

"I know what I asked and I know how you answered," Owen responded.

"I trust my intuition for my own decisions and I like sharing it with you and teaching you about it but I don't have the confidence to contribute to this level of consequences," I shared.

We all were in the fly bridge navigating out of the inlet, when Owen directed, "Bimini."

"Bimini?" Captain balked with both surprise and disgust.

"Yes, we are going there now," he said with no further explanation.

We rode quietly for the better part of the southwest trek towards Bimini.

Owen pointed towards the sky, "Look, the clouds have formed a big marlin shape in the sky."

Captain was about to pop, "So, you want to target marlin today? Tuna again? What are we fishing for today? You want to fish around Bimini?"

"You two are dropping me off at Bimini Blue Water Resort, then you will fish long and hard and have fun and head back to Boat Harbor. Call me Sunday at noon sharp from your phone. Get my phone, too, that I bagged up in Boat Harbor, but don't turn it on. You have to trust me Ed. Just do what I say today," Owen said.

I noticed he addressed him as Ed and not Captain. Captains rule on the seas in a boat. In this case, Owen clearly was in charge.

"Are you meeting people there? Do you need our help? Should we stay with you?" I asked.

"No. We need to separate. You or "we" are still fishing and heading back to Boat Harbor. The GPS on my phone is still signaling there at the marina. If we've been followed, we are still moving and fishing. Don't worry, you are safe here on the boat. I have cameras and will know every move should you get in trouble. I have a top secret classified matter to deal with in Bimini. You will know all about it in two days," he assured, quietly facing me directly where Captain could not hear over the wind and motor noises.

We pulled into the dredged canal around the island of Bimini. The manmade canal struck an unnatural chord among the flow of mega-nature of the islands. Captain and I didn't even get off the boat. Owen ran downstairs, directing us to stay on the fly bridge, waved goodbye and hopped off onto the marina dock. He disappeared into the two room building before we pulled away. Bimini is the closest to Florida, just an hour by boat to Ft. Lauderdale, so I assumed Owen was being picked up to get back to the States to work on the oil issue.

We motored back through the canal to the open waters and pointed towards Boat Harbor. In the back of the boat, in the water spraying up from the sides, I saw another rainbow. At least the rainbows were back.

I could feel my starfish dangle earrings whipping against my neck in the wind. My hair was loose, not in a ponytail. I'd never get out all the tangles. I thought about what I wanted for lunch. Think about anything but Owen's predicament! I wanted to be out to lunch. Checked out. Or I wanted some answers. Either knowing everything or nothing at all would be preferable to this in between cross currents of mental friction.

CHAPTER 8, HACKED WITH SPYWARE LAST SUMMER

"Hey, Captain, now that Owen's gone, I want to update you on the freaky events that happened to me last summer. I have a restraining order against a guy and he weekends a lot in Boat Harbor. Owen knows about the whole big hairy ordeal and since Owen's not here, you should know in case the guy pops up somewhere. I don't think he's dangerous, but I can't be one-hundred percent sure," I said.

I settled into the other swivel seat and raised my voice to carry over the wind and engine sounds.

"Do you remember Rick, the computer security expert whiz guy? He joined us at the Palm Beach marina bar a few times? He dealt with the uber-wealthy on cyber security of their investments?" I asked.

"The New York big mouth nerd with the spray tan and fake teeth? And what's up with those girl hair-highlights he has?" he asked.

Rick was clean cut and always dressed to the nines in Ralph Lauren down to his Stubbs & Wootten slippers. He was Tom-Cruise-type model looking, just a wee bit too short. He was way too muscular and way too tan and way to sales-savvy to be a true legitimate computer nerd. He didn't have a slide rule or pocket protector, but he did have an arsenal of iPhones at all times. He spent too much time on the beach and in the Palm Beach bar circuit, and not enough in an office, to be earning the amount of money he was spending.

"Well, New York, yes, I met him at Bull and Bear two years ago but he's in Palm Beach now. He rented a house in SoSo, south of Southern Boulevard in West Palm Beach. We were both moving our businesses to Palm Beach, so he seemed friendly and affable enough, so we mingled around some about the island," I said.

"That guy's too short for you. He's cheap; leaves terrible tips. And he drinks sissy drinks. You can't trust a man that you can't have a real drink with," spouted Captain.

"Really? C'mon. I wasn't dating the guy. He was an acquaintance. He was new to the area, just like I was. He was Gordon-good-guy at first blush. He hung out with me always in groups, never just us two. Man, I'm trying to tell you a story," I snapped.

"It was a shark attack. I didn't see it coming. A big group was having dinner at the community table at Buccan. Rick said his battery was low in his phone and asked to borrow my phone. He stepped outside with both phones and was gone for 15 minutes. I went outside to find him with thumbs flying all over my phone. I snatched it from him, but obviously too late. He put spyware on my iPhone. The easiest way to tell is that the battery dies quickly because another program is running behind in the background. If you look it up online, you'll see spyware for sale all over the internet. It's rampant. Anyway, the next day I called him and I told him to undo whatever he had done and we'd walk away friends. Then the following day, he sent me an e-mail apology with an attachment, and I'm so stupid, I opened it and it unleashed spyware all in my Macs, and it ruined my life for a few months and scared the hell out of me. I hate the guy," I summarized.

"Let's pulverize him into one of these buckets and use him for bait. Done," Captain snapped.

"Ha! That's the solution Owen said you would have. By the way, I'm worried about Owen," I said.

"I'm worried that I'll end up paranoid and skit-zy like you two. You need to lighten up. Owen's always secretive and sneaking and peeking around places. He likes to explore on his own. The guy is a cat with nine lives. He could survive anything. He's OK. He's always OK," Captain said.

"Yeah," I shrugged.

I didn't really mean I believed Owen was OK. I didn't believe we were OK. Or that the world was OK. It was like in this little bubble of the world, on this little boat, Owen was the big marlin trying to avert disaster, and I represented the communicators – the media and such, and Captain was the masses, happily skipping along with normal life oblivious to any danger, just focused on the fuel gauge and the horizon. And in the meantime, didn't Owen say the boat itself probably had a big, fat target on it from the bad guys? Really, where is Owen?

"Hey, are you the reason I had to leave my iPhone at the marina office?" asked Captain.

"I'm not sure exactly what that was all about. It makes me feel not as safe, being unable to communicate by phone, but we have the VHF here on the boat," I said.

We chased some birds and raised two wahoo. Captain fileted them right as they were caught. I never liked to see the fish flesh put into Baggies in the freezer before they have time to fully die. Poor fish. I couldn't look. I felt like I could hear the ripping of the blade under the scales, but I couldn't really. My senses were in total overload.

Captain came back up the stairs and, as always after finding fish, punched in the location on the GPS.

"No!" I screamed.

"No?" Captain asked shaking his head stunned at my outburst.

"Well, maybe Owen didn't want anyone to know our exact location and that's why he had us leave our phones and computers," I offered.

"You have got to chill sista'. No sketchy bad guys or spies around here unless they are in a submarine," he said and gestured arms extended to the expansive horizon with bright blue skies dotted with a few puffy clouds.

He lit a Lucky Strike and drew in a big breath and let out a huge stream of smoke that blew over the back of the boat over all the equipment and lingered over the fuel intake. I wondered if with flammable diesel below us, and the wind blowing fire from his ciggie all over, if boats ever lit up like atomic bombs on the high seas.

"Speaking of submarine, I could use lunch. I have lunch for us in the 'fridge from Zorba's. They make a great gyro sub. While Owen's on the boat, I stock up on groceries on his dime. We've got oranges and my favorite Bar-be-que chips. Help yourself down there," he said.

Captain was with Owen on all of his trips. He travelled all the time with him. I was never sure exactly how much Owen confided in him, but this was crystal clear that Captain Ed had no idea what a mess we were in. It was probably best for him to stay focused on driving the boat and getting us back to land. I'd like to get off this floating target myself. He didn't have a big attention span even if you wanted to give him more details. I tried to picture Captain back in the radio station offices where he worked before he escaped to life in Captain land, or sea I should say. I looked at his face under the baseball cap and sunglasses, with his brown hair just a little too long for corporate life, and skin much more weathered than if he

34

had cubicle-ed it for a career. You could probably get him back in a suit and tie, but the lack of freedom that he has now would be a big shocker. I wondered to myself whatever would this man do now if Owen lost it. "It"meaning everything, not just the boat.

"Birds! They're diving low. There's fish there. Dinner! Woo-hoo!" laughed Captain with his boy-ish exuberance every time he dropped a line. He never seemed to bore of fishing after all these years.

Lines down. Bite. Down to reel. The fish took out another 50 feet before I could get down to the reel. The fish was strong and pulling determined to win our tug-of-war game. I set in on my own goal to win and reeled using the weight of my whole body. Then he gave up. Just like that, he stopped fighting. I reeled the 200 feet in quickly.

"Rotten robber sharks took our 'hoo," Captain screamed from above. He could see the fish head bobbing from his vantage point.

As Captain came down to toss the head to the predators, too, and reel in the lines, I thought fishing really wasn't unlike the business world. With just a small bit of blood from a tiny hook, a shark can smell the blood and attack the easy prey. They aren't being bad; it is a shark's job to take out the injured or dying so the rest of the school isn't held back by the weak. The shark was just being a shark. So, like in 'hoo-ville at sea, we make choices and choices make us. Stay with the school and keep swimming. Take the bait, bleed, and attract sharks. You might shake loose the hook and live, but now injured, might get eaten anyway, or boated, for sure a goner. Basically, taking the bait increases staggering statistics that you've put yourself in harm's way. Owen took the bait. He signed the deceptive contract. I wondered how he would get out of it; or if he could get out of it.

CHAPTER 9, PHISHING TRIP-UP

Captain knew all he needed to know. I gave up on trying to share any more details with him. Some people would be enthralled when I'd share the spyware tale, and others didn't want to be bothered. Captain clearly didn't care. The whirr of the motor and balmy wind, combined with total lack of sleep, lulled me into deep thought. I had brought the consciousness of last summer into my mind, something I had worked hard to push back into the depths of memory into a category named, "My Past I'd Like To Forget."

In an episode of the TV series *Allie McBeal*, Allie claimed something like, "I don't think my problems are bigger than anyone else's. They are just my problems and that is what makes them big to me."

My problem, when brought to light, seemed pretty solvable. I had one identifiable creepy pervert and a technical issue to solve. Just hire "a guy" to fix it. Then the problems really began with who to hire and the reality of how very vulnerable we all are. There is no go-to "guy" and there is no solution.

I'm at that age where three-martini-lunches in media were replaced right at the time I started my career with serious software and measureable data and digital production. As a marketing person, I liked that I could create data-driven ad campaigns, rather than the old Darren Stevens method. It was fun to create websites and show clients how many hits it got on each page, how long each person stayed on each page, where they clicked to next, who bought; it was fun like a video game. I don't consider myself a technical person but it's a necessary evil to being successful. There was always an IT person with my associated businesses, so I never learned how to load the software or update it or troubleshoot technical issues.

So, I quickly found I have the proverbial elephant to eat. How? One bite at a time, of course is the advice. In my case a giant killer whale just swam down the haunted hall in *The Shining*. Get your spoons out team!

The gist is that Rick got access to my iPhone, then he accessed my Mac Pro with an executable program attached that I opened. He wrote me an apology e-mail and it had an attachment. I was so stupid that I opened it. I was curious and as I clicked on the attachment, I lost control of the Mac. No keys worked. I couldn't turn it off. A Word software update pop-up menu came on the monitor. It wasn't really a Word update only looked like one, and I watched as my username and password for the Mac wrote themselves into the blanks. As I watched evil take over my monitor and install itself, without me being able to push any key to stop it, I immediately realized my pathetic plight.

I think I'm smart enough to avoid Phishing scams, which is social engineering to get information by using fake e-mails, websites or other electronic communication. First of all, I don't even have time to open files unless they are part of my business day. He already had my username and password because I stored it on the iPhone so I'd have it when I travelled. He must have already installed a gotomypc. com type of program because he froze me out and took over the whole thing while he installed the phishing Word update fraudulent malware.

Since he was targeting me with his guise, he was spear-phishing. He speared me and the sharks were circling.

I've spear fished enough to know, you get your bounty in the boat quickly because sharks will smell the blood and follow quickly behind the kill to scavenge any leftover fish. What would follow this action? My guess is he created the software and was testing it on me, perhaps others, since he was, after all, a computer programmer.

Watching the Mac infect itself with spyware, without me being able to do one thing about it, other than photograph the fiasco, left me terrorized, and more angry than I have ever known myself to be. It must be what European citizens felt when Hitler took over their homes, or when Trujillo took Dominican businesses, and this evil electronic dictator, without my permission and against my will, just stole my peace within my home and my business.

I had put my whole life in the Mac in preparation of being an empty nester with world travels. I had just in the last 90 days set up online banking, Paypal, Square, Skype, Dragon Dictate, Dropbox, and all updated software in the Adobe Suite. I moved all records and documents to data rather than just paper, and kept an organized Word document in a folder called "AAA" my personal file right at the top of my document file with an alphabetical list of every online everything in my life with user names and passwords. Every username and password to my entire life would be the very first file an electronic thief would find. It's like I left my mother's jewelry and all my cash sitting by my front door so even the Domino's delivery guy could grab a handful. I would normally describe myself as intelligent, creative, organized and Type A. I changed my adjective at that moment to just plain stupid, so, so, so stupid.

CHAPTER 10, SEA OF PEOPLE

Last summer, I hired a bunch of people to help and quickly ruled out the ones that in the first hour said, "You are so paranoid," or "Just change your passwords," or "Just buy new computers." Nothing was a "just" but rather an unchartered mysterious sequence.

I started first by hiring a private detective to make sure Rick wasn't an ax murderer and that I wasn't in physical danger. The first thing he told me was, "Stay off your phone and your computers until we can get to the bottom of this incident."

"Really? Do you know how much I depend upon these devices? I run my whole life from them," I responded but tried to go back to old-fashioned chicken scratch handwriting.

I didn't know why Rick had done this. He had a stalker creep-factor to him. He was a handsome guy and could buy drinks and get attractive women to talk to him but he couldn't snag a girlfriend. He would tell me he wanted a girlfriend, so when I was in town in Palm Beach, I'd introduce him to people I knew. I speculated maybe he was gay and pretending to want a steady girlfriend. Who knows with this guy?

I had asked him for a month or so if he had spyware on my phone because he would meet me and other friends for an after dinner drink, and he would join in on the conversation as though he had been at The Palm Beach Grill with us. "So, you are from Michigan," he would ask someone with me he had never met. Creepy at night. He would text, "I'm at Starbucks. Where are you?" when I'd be in my Palm Beach condo with a friend talking about needing a caffeine kick-start at Starbucks. Creepy in the morning. He would always know when I was coming to Palm Beach before I told him. He kept two or three phones with him at all times and tinkered with them constantly like a nervous twitch. He was doing suspect spyware-type actions more and more frequently. He seemed to get confused about what he should know from direct conversations, and what he listened to spying on me that he shouldn't know. In interactions with him, Rick was slipping in his communication as part of conversations we really had in each other's presence, and also conversations he had observed from afar. Well, not too far, the phone on my ear, in my purse, on my desk, or beside my bed. The phone, and therefore Rick, both were with me always.

I didn't rule out psychic ability as his quirk. I'm intuitive but don't use my gift as a way to stalk people. I ruled out this possibility with him because when I asked several times, "So, where are you spiritually?"

Rick answered, "I grew up Catholic. I'm agnostic now."

That answer scares me under any circumstance. That answer was common among the self-made, self-sufficient, success-driven set, so not unusual. That answer does rule out someone who has spiritual awareness though. So, I was back to "Just the facts, ma'am."

The private detective came highly recommended by Owen but he wasn't tech savvy. He was one of those guys with first names for his first and last like John Scott, or Bob David, or Michael Pat. I loaded "Detective" in my iPhone with four of his numbers. He had a lot of numbers. He had a potbelly, beige garb, conservatively cut curly gray hair and dark sunglasses. He drove several non-descript four-door sedans to our meetings.

One of his first questions was, "Do you have an Apple or a Mac?"

I actually had a PC, too. I had lots of computers and lots of problems. We both acknowledged that he could do the background search, but we'd need a computer expert to help us unravel the beast. I wanted proof, too. I wanted Rick to go to jail. It was criminal what he was doing.

"The background search didn't show up any criminal activity," Detective told me, "But that doesn't mean he didn't commit crimes. He just didn't get caught. And dead people don't tell on you. He still could be dangerous so we need to tread lightly. He's making great money and has a rental in Palm Beach County. He owns a black 2010 Audi. He got divorced five years ago and the wife took nothing and got nothing and moved to Los Angeles. It's strange to me that he's making all this money and it appears from the non-contested court records that she just wanted out and wanted to get away from this guy. I could go to L.A. and interview her. Ex-spouses are a great resource for securing leads for information. I'd have to charge you and it could be expensive. You might be better off as a woman-to-woman to call her and level with her and ask her straight-up if you are in danger with this guy," Detective suggested.

My first thought burst out, "I wonder what he did to her to scare her so much? I doubt she'll talk. She's probably elated he's moved his addiction, obsession, control or whatever to a new victim. Do people like that really help others?"

He moved on to the nitty-gritty of the technical investigation.

Detective only wanted me to work with his computer people. That made sense given the nature of my security issue. I wasted several weeks waiting for return calls from computer gurus and forensic experts. Most of them told me they couldn't work on Macs, only PCs. If I did get a meeting with them, they'd spend the first half hour telling me how smart they were and the second half hour telling me to buy new computers and confirming that, yes, a bad guy could get right back in to new ones. Then they'd bill me their hourly fee of $100 to $300 for their expertise.

Some of the men didn't want to get tangled in my legal issues. Interestingly there was not one woman. I wondered if a woman would deal with a stalker victim in a different way than these men.

I called Owen exasperated in the middle of a mass of meetings, "Is there not a person among us who can fight this monster? These guys want to avoid personal accountability and not take a stand to protect our basic rights to communicate with free speech, basic rights to privacy, and ownership of our own identities, which are all at serious risk. Sue-happy people and TV commercials with get-rich-quick off Mr. Big 800 numbers have dulled the quick responses of the capable to protect, to be a voice, to man-up. I need to find someone with some balls. Pardon my French."

I vented some to Owen because, number one, he was my business mentor and, number two, he was my client. I wasn't billing him because I couldn't work on my projects because I couldn't use my Mac. I wanted him to know why I wasn't performing my tasks and that I had it under control. I needed my freelance contract with him and didn't want him to replace me with some upcoming deadlines that were looming. I was losing money every day this dragged out. I could lose a little money, but I couldn't afford to lose my largest client.

I interviewed layers of local corporate expert IT guys from a bank, a hospital, a law firm. I learned to interview them on the phone rather than scheduling and waiting for a meeting after hours, only to find out they couldn't help me and I'd have to pay their one-hour minimum freelance fee. Their fees were mounting and my business checking account was shrinking. The corporate IT guys living in the safety of 401Ks and lackadaisical malaise, didn't know spyware existed, and would knee-jerk argue that it couldn't be installed on a Mac. Where Apple failed in keeping up with security measures, they excelled in corporate PR. America bought wholly the idea that Macs are safe.

During this ordeal, I realized how much I was reliant upon my Mac because I didn't want to build my arsenal of data and proof and have the bad guy read it online. I created it all handwritten, then 3-hole punched the papers and stored them in a stack of binders, and then copied all the pages. I didn't rule out that everything I copied could be duplicated elsewhere, but it was a risk I took. I'd copy the files in other offices when I could.

I took photos of anything creepy appearing on the phone or computers since the camera was a separate device and not linked to the computers in any way. I spent a lot of time at CVS Pharmacy printing photos and making back up CDs of the photo disc in the camera. The sales clerk memorized not only my name, but my phone number and address, too. She knew the first few digits of my frequent buyer number. I was in there a lot.

The clerk told me several times, "I hope you bring in vacation photos to be processed soon and get to take some time off work."

I agreed with her. A break would be welcomed.

The basic advice from most sources was to change passwords on the router, and in each computer. The cable company put in last name as my username and phone number as password so I had no security at all through the router. When I called the cable company for them to walk me through how to change it, I asked why they used such simple passwords. They explained so their technicians can work from your driveway if you need repairs, and they don't have to come inside because it's common knowledge what the passwords and usernames are.

CHAPTER 11, SPYWARE SHARK AND ALLIGATOR ATTACK

I went downstairs to the cooler, got a bottled water, and came back up with Captain on the boat to continue my daydream about last summer. Maybe in the quiet expanse of the sea, I would sense a solution. If I just meditated and sat still for long enough, maybe I could "get" the answer.

In the painfully long wait for help last May and June, I started looking around in my own computers to document to make the repair process go faster.

I started with the Mac Pro. I found Unix executable files in the trash. I threw away files that I didn't use that kept popping up on my desktop like Image Capture, Panorama Maker, Photo Booth and such, and alias duplicates of all kinds of everything. Everything I did generated two icons on the desktop.

I Googled a few times and found more terrifying data of how simple it is for someone to pretend like they are you and manipulate your computer remotely. I found advice on blogs for something called Remote Tap. There were many other remote access programs but I don't remember their names.

On iMac desktop, with a glass of wine one night, I sat down at the built-in desk in the kitchen. I was becoming more and more isolated, because joining friends for a glass of wine out for happy hour, I would just obsess over my issue. I wasn't very good company.

I left the computers on all the time including this iMac. I rarely used it. It had been used by a series of assistants, interns and freelancers when I had an office and now sat still between occasional freelancers. It basically was a digital file cabinet to me of past documents.

I pulled down the apple icon menu, to recent items, servers, Team. I don't have a server called "Team." I went to start up disc, Mac, Network Startup and there it was "Team." I took a quick photo, I clicked on it and the monitor lit up and went dark four times then a message "Connection Failed" then the Mac went dark and turned itself off.

After a few minutes, I got it to come back on. I changed the password from "creepBgone" to "StayAwayU2." I had already changed it once but he must have been watching and changed it on his end, too. I unclicked in the "Team" file "allow user to administer" in preferences. I turned off the file sharing and printer sharing functions. We had never shared printers, each Mac had a dedicated printer attached with a cable, so I wasn't sure why this was on. I didn't even have an HP printer at all. I went back to the menu to Apple, Recent Items, Servers, AraxiHome and AraxiPreps were the named servers that turned on and "Team" duplicated every function of the iMac in real time in a remote location. I was able to get to this while he was scrambling to get the new password I just put in. I took photos of every step as evidence. I was shaking. I turned off the iMac. I unplugged it.

I stood back and stared at it for a few minutes with my arms crossed. I realized "he" was different than Rick. This was creep number two, technically number one, since "he" was probably there since the one terrible assistant who probably installed it or allowed it to happen. I realized every conversation I had both personal and business was watched from the camera at the top of the monitor. In the phone conversations, "he" could hear my end. Since I closed my office space several months prior in the process of creating my total virtual office, "he" now lived in my kitchen.

It could be that "he" saw Rick sliding the slippery slope labeled as the cyber criminal and "he" took the opportunity to create cyber chaos while there was another person to blame it on. I named this second creep "Sick." So, now I have Rick and Sick.

So, Rick was the shark attack and Sick is the alligator attack. The difference is the shark takes a bite, rips some flesh, doesn't like the taste of human meat, so he swims away. An alligator has a whole different approach to dining. He clamps down on a limb, then he spins into a death roll where the victim is underwater and totally dizzy and disoriented. He takes the limb if it rips off, or the whole victim, and shoves it under a log underwater to tenderize it and flavor it. He comes back to feast later. The pungent smell and taste of rotten flesh pleases his palette. Both prehistoric predators can be deadly, but the alligator is the worst of the two. Sick was the alligator.

I have the iMac I kept for criminal evidence but never turned it on again. It sits on a shelf in my storage room, which used to be a fourth bedroom, with the printer beside it, frozen in time.

On the other Macs, I put a Post-it note over the camera on the top of the monitor so I couldn't be filmed. I asked every computer expert I talked to how to stop the cameras from working, and they all recommended basic cover the lens techniques. I later learned I had covered the camera just a little too late.

CHAPTER 12, SPYWARE SHARK BITE VICTIMS

Last summer, Rick or Sick or something or someone shifted his malicious daily terror from the shared iMac, to my Mac Pro. I had Ann come over that afternoon. She had briefly dated the person who I thought could be Sick and I recalled some story about stalking. She told me horror stories of how he put spyware on her computer and terrorized her for a year after she stopped dating him. She said he would assume being her and construct detrimental documents and e-mails under her identity. She brought her files to show me how she documented proof that it was Sick so I could see how to document my stalkers.

On the Mac, I turned up Pandora to the maximum volume, I turned off the iPhone and put it beside the blaring music, and we whispered on the other side of the room. Supposedly with spyware, when you turn the phone off, it just becomes a microphone and camera, the spyware never turns off. Pandora shut itself down three times during our meeting. We moved the meeting to Houston's. I needed a Chardonnay. We settled into the Adirondack chairs out by the lake under the oaks.

As empathetic as she was, even with her being a past victim of spyware herself, she asked, "Are you sure you aren't being paranoid?"

"Really? What? Weren't you just in the same room with me with the computer operating itself?" I asked.

"Yes. You just need to be very sure because it's the first question people ask. You as the victim become the person in question before they ever get to the bad guys. I got tired of it. So tired. I hope you stick with it and stick it to him. I'm behind you one-hundred percent," Ann said.

"You are sounding one-hundred percent wimpy and spineless," I said.

"You know I was creeped-out when Sicko put spyware on my computer. He's sick but not bright. He'd pretend he was me in e-mails, then accidentally in the e-mail chain, he would send it from his e-mail address. Print out the e-mail and here's black and white proof of his covert actions. The guy is an idiot. A vengeful, twisted idiot, so I'm glad I'm out of his bubble. Your nickname 'Sick' for him is perfect," Ann toasted to the setting sun and sipped her red wine.

"Spyware is wrong but it's online for as low as nineteen-bucks so it happens all the time in business and personal relationships. Remember when I first got separated, I had set up all the usernames and passwords for all of our online finances. My ex wasn't very techie so I had access to the online banking including real time charges I could view on his credit card. Remember when I would get pissed when he'd be taking little chickies to pricey Victoria and Albert and not paying child support on time? And I would see his Sun Pass charges with him checking into the airport parking and also tolls to Miami to play with girls half his age? I could get into his calendar at his office, too. All he had to do was set up his own username and password and he could have kept me out of his private matters. Since he never set up usernames and passwords, and if he did, he used only our son's name and birthday each time, I could spy on him anytime. I didn't really look at that like spying but really it was I suppose. I was invisible because I just looked. The difference with Sick is that he became active and malicious in his cyber presence with me. Are they both wrong? Well, maybe," she said.

"Well, how would you feel if roles were reversed and your ex was checking our bar tab now?" I asked.

"You know, spying on your ex is pretty harmless. We know each other. We were married. What you are dealing with is pure terror. You don't know these people you have spying on you. You don't know what they are capable of. You spent how much did you say, $5,000 just this week on private investigators and computer experts? I care about you and I'm concerned about you. You need to just stay put here for a while. Why do you have to go to South Florida all the time? You must have been a nomad in a prior life," Ann lectured.

"South Florida isn't the problem. The world is. My problem isn't geographically defined, it's omnipotent like the air. Besides, look at the lake here Ann. I love that in one glance we are seeing every shore, the baby ducks, and the little turtle heads popping up. But in this little inland lily pad oasis, the fish are limited to only that between the shores of the lake. They are land locked and trapped. Coastal communities have massive reefs accessible to international

shores with daily tides delivering massive fish in and out continu-
ally. Safe is boring. Travel is titillating. It's stimulating. I like the
culture and art in Palm Beach, and each little beach town around
the Florida coast. I feel spiritually drawn to Palm Beach, something I'll tell you about some other time. And I found a hot Ted-
fish in the Keys. When was your last hot date here in Mayberry?" I
asked.

"That's not fair. There are fun dates here," she retorted.

"You are recycling high school prom dates. Look, here I tell
people I'm a writer and the first thing they suggest is, 'You should
write about the housewives of our town.' Really? Really? Read
Cosmo sometime and look at the stats. Bi-sexual, bi-racial, bipolar,
nothing is shocking in the big world beyond our village. Affairs
aren't novel, sex isn't in short supply, and that's about the raci-
est thing going around here. Besides, when I don't think you
and I would have the starring roles in local gossip paperbacks,
I'll get right on that writing assignment. Uh, not. Nobody cares
beyond our zip code about who is dancing in whose kitchen with
the blinds closed. The only people who care are the other people
in the triangles. Mostly here it's complicated trapezoids, with all
the love child half siblings of married moms and dads running
around. Our stories are provincial and small. It's only interesting if it involves something funny that we jest with to entertain
ourselves. It's only memorable if it involves punches thrown in
public or cars crashed through buildings. Maybe we could do all
of Orlando and include the celebs on the west side. Even then, I
can't remember the names or places or details of any of the news,
not even the high profile people. I'm not much of a gossip anyway; it's not my style. I find my own life is full and rich and if I'm
taking the time to spend with someone, I generally think they are
interesting, so want to hear about their life," I said.

"The local stories are juicy and you could sell millions then have
a mansion on Palm Beach Island instead of a rental condo there,"
said Ann.

"What would happen is I'd get sued for millions of dollars by
the people who thought I was telling their tales. They would all
think I'm talking about them! Lots of people keep a secret. And

everyone has what they think is a secret, that isn't a secret at all," I laughed.

"I find more interesting people and topics out in the world. You can sit at the bar at Bice or Taboo on Worth Avenue, or at Green's Pharmacy for coffee, and the world comes to you. You can just sit on the reef and meet high rollers and bi-polars, and everything in between. You can't fully experience life through the TV or internet. I'm a five-senses girl. I like the texture of all the cotton and linen resort-wear clothes. I like to smell the 18-year scotch on their breath when they brag about their summer homes on the Cape and yachts in the Mediterranean," I explained.

"If you want gossip, at least make it world-class. For momentary entertainment and inspiration for characters, you can listen to the whispered snippets from the tan scantily clad model-looking girls at Cucina, the restaurant turned nightclub after dinner. You learn the truth and the lies about every man in the room if you stand next to a few girl packs. 'He's married from Boca and takes his ring off.' ... 'He's the ultimate Palm Beach player and gave my friend a disease. Ewwww.' ... 'He's got a house on the island and put a drug in my drink.' ... 'He is bankrupt and right out of federal prison for being a con.' ... So, you learn a lot in short order about this little segment of the world, maybe it's true or not, but it's entertaining and harmless. I don't believe it unless I get to know the person and find out for myself. I wouldn't repeat any of it and I certainly wouldn't write about it. Gossip isn't meant to be in print. I like to fill my brain with more important data. I do like to observe it then reflect on the essence of the interactions on my several hour drive home after beach trips. The rhythm of chaos then quiet suits me as a creative person," I said.

"I do like to watch the flush of red on their cheeks when they hand me a cheesy, phony business card, and my intuition kicks in, and my mouth opens and I challenge them lightly and watch them squirm. I was mortified when I Googled the one and he had a laundry list of international crimes. He didn't find my intuition so humorous. I avoided him until he victimized his prey and moved to a new city. Remember me telling you about that guy?" I said.

"Yes, this is what I'm talking about! Mayberry has a sheriff and deputy on duty. Keep your digits in Mayberry! Stay put here, Charlotte," she said.

"We live in the digital world. Safety and danger live in equal parts anywhere in the world now. Remember another time when I was in Palm Beach again and I got the call from the security department of my bank about my Visa being used 'out of my normal shopping' at a Walmart in Sanford? Data is black and white wherever you roam, so the bank quickly stopped the criminal shoppers who pirated my credit card, and the bank stopped me from being charged. Now, would my card have been more vulnerable in Palm Beach to scammers of all types and cyber criminals? Maybe. The point is, that digital danger can start and stop anywhere at anytime. Palm Beach has the word 'beach' in it, so that is my main attraction to it," I pondered.

"Here is the thing, Ann, we have an epidemic of apathy in our society now. Look at you, since you survived a spyware episode and you 'innocently' spied on your ex, you are numb to how much danger we face. I feel this intense sense of alarm and I can't even communicate it to you, my best friend, face-to-face. It's like there is no word in the English language to communicate what I want to scream to the world right now. Maybe a tribe in Zambia has a word used for when an enormous wild animal is rushing at you and death is imminent within seconds. That is the word I would use if I knew what it was," I said.

"The bottom line is, we are in trouble and we are asleep sitting here in our dripping diamonds and designer wear and sipping California wines by a lake. This utopia that evolved in the last 200 years, called capitalistic America, built on a spirit of work ethic and freedom and God and unity and charity and civility is in danger. Do you understand? I am afraid that my stalker might kill me, yes, but my bigger fear is that our entire civilized society, as we know it and enjoy it, is in terrible jeopardy. Unscrupulous international criminal minds can wipe out our infrastructure and bring us to a third-world scavenger survival-mode. They can do it in an instant, totally invisible and virtually untraceable, from anywhere in the world. They are most likely to do it where illegal activities are already their way of life, where they don't share the same values and morals as us, not even close. Think about what Hurricane Charley did to Florida and picture a computer virus shutting down our utilities. Picture a drug lord with that power in his laptop. It's possible. Think about the threat of the Y2K virus at the millennium and all that we feared might happen if computers shut down. The digital world didn't self-implode midnight striking the year 2000 as predicted in Y2K, but technology still is both our friend and our enemy," I continued.

"You are a big downer today. Let's get your computers fixed and get you cheered up. You are bumming me out. This isn't like you," said Ann.

We got our checks and I paid cash. I changed my purchase behavior to start using cash more, so Rick couldn't trace my whereabouts from watching my credit card transactions.

The sun was setting and it was time to get our cars from the valet. I hopped in my BMW and popped in a CD. I still keep faves around. The Dixie Chicks sang me my theme song from *The Long Way Around* with my windows down to feel the cooling night air, "Well, I never seem to do it like anybody else, Maybe someday, someday I'm gonna' settle down, If you ever want me I can still be found, Taking the long way around ..."

CHAPTER 13, NEW PHONE IS POSSESSED

After Ann's cavalier attitude towards spyware, I gave up and decided to replace my phone rather than trying to document the spying. The next day after meeting with her, at the AT&T Store I got a new iPhone and new phone number so I could have private conversations. Except for my children, I didn't give the new number to anyone. My phone number spelled my name and I had given the number out for fifteen years. In one instant, I would become a disconnected number to literally thousands of contacts. I would just have to find my friends and business contacts again when things settled down. I had no choice. I blocked my new number so when I called people, the caller ID would say "blocked." I forwarded my office number to my cell so my clients could still contact me. I spent an hour with the sales guy turning off anything that wasn't absolutely necessary and going over every single safety feature. I learned some photo tricks, too, which made the arduous afternoon somewhat fun.

At 4:30 a.m. the phone came to life like Chuckie in *Magic* and "Click. Click. Ding. Ding." the Network file in the Settings was open and someone was remotely installing a Personal Hotspot. I sat straight up in bed, screamed my head off, freaked out and hit the data delete function wiping the phone back to factory settings.

I took the photos and the story into the manager of the AT&T Store the next morning. He wrote it down for me since I was so scared I could barely listen and hear his explanation. "A personal hotspot makes the phone a wireless modem which allows the phone to connect computers to the phone to use the internet."

The manager was creeped out, too, and gave me a discount on yet another new iPhone and another new phone number. He said we could wipe that one back to factory settings but it was to be another paperweight in my techie-graveyard at my home office. The manager said to tether from a mobile hot spot, he would have to have a data plan, so if I let the creep set up the hot spot next time, we could probably trace him to his data plan.

So, now in 24 hours, I wiped out my simple to remember cell phone number that I had for over fifteen years. Clients, friends, family members would ring that number and not reach me. I didn't even want to start giving out my new number because look at what happened to the first new number that lasted less than 24 hours. I was becoming more and more isolated, alone, and helpless. As an accomplished, capable person, the computer issues were changing my behavior and also how I saw myself. It was an interesting, yet disturbing, experience.

During this time, I had intense recurring dreams, creating extreme sleep deprivation. I didn't want to sleep if these were my dreams of men in armor, and the underworld, and battles of every century on every continent. I'd wake each morning and try to doze back off for a minute like re-booting a computer to try to change my facts on my mental monitor. The lack of sleep compounded with the intense problem solving, caused a self-diagnosed mild depression. Like the little scratch on my Chanel sunglasses, that I can't wipe clean, and each wipe leaves a different layer of a dull film, obstructing the clarity and light.

Since I wasn't going out as much, and I sat glued for hours Google-ing forums and sites to find solutions, I put on a few pounds, ten in two months. I had never, ever done that before in my whole life. So, now I was going to be a chubby, depressed, scared, paranoid victim? No. I refused. I fought it.

Time heals and mercifully I have erased much of the details of last summer but one occurrence is embedded in my very conscious mind forever.

So, now I wasn't really sure if the creeps plural or singular were listening from one of the Macs or the phone but I had to have serious help. Not Deputy Dawg, the private eye who was trying, but in effect just taking up time and letting the problem worsen.

All the creepy things that were happening were getting worse. Whenever I was getting advice on the phone or in person, the Mac Pro would interact and get my attention by flashing different screen savers. When I would walk over, it would return to the ocean wave screen saver I had chosen. Sometimes the music site Pandora would start itself and give me messages in the lyrics. My airline reservations and travel plans were always placed on my screen desktop even though I had not taken them from the e-mail file. I could not turn on my computers or wake them without some random screen saver stalling my access to my own Mac and communicating some disturbing message. After a few weeks, the cyber creep or creeps wouldn't even bother to hide their tracks. "He" would leave whatever he was pilfering through right on the desktop with the file open. I could go into recent items and see where he had been. I could open the trash to see what he put there. I killed lots of trees within a few weeks printing everything in my existing files and all of the bizarre occurrences, and filed it in my home office. The stacks of paper were overwhelming if nothing else. I went through lots of $35 ink cartridges. I bought the volume bulk packages. The chaos was making me crazy.

On my brand new phone, I called Owen hysterical by now and asked what to do and who to call.

Owen said, "Immediately call my in-house attorney and tell him that Rick is committing a federal offense because he is interfering in international commerce over the phone, over the computers, and it is affecting your business. Call the FBI. Call my personal CIA tech guy that I just used to set up my iPad. He's a smart son-of-a-bitch. Let's get to the bottom of this and get back to being productive."

During this conversation, the screen savers went crazy on the Mac

Pro that I had set up on the kitchen counter. I stood up and worked in the kitchen a lot. When people met at my home office, we sat on the kitchen counter bar stools often. The iMac camera at the top of the monitor could also see and film two Pier One counter height tables with chairs where sometimes up to ten of us met, and the dining room table where eight would meet. It was in the center of a huge great room where I worked. My clients said my home was so peaceful and quiet, not like the hub of a real office, and one called it "the think tank" and another "the idea factory." It was also the personal space after 5 p.m., for me, and for my dear family.

The screen savers displayed Word-of-the-day dictionary messages. I read them aloud to Owen, "Attenuate. Verb. Reduce the force, effect or value of. Reduce the amplitude of such as of a signal, electrical current, or other oscillation. Adj. Attenuated. Reduce the virulence of such as of a pathogenic organism or vaccine. Reduce in thickness. Make thin."

Another screen popped up and I read it aloud, "Wrath. Noun. Extreme anger chiefly used for humorous or rhetorical effect."

Another screen saver popped up as I finished reading that one and again, I read it aloud, "Westering. Adj. especially of the sun nearing the west."

"Oh my God! Is this a threat? Am I in danger? This has to stop! Help me," I cried out to Owen on the phone.

I looked in the reflection of the Mac monitor sitting on my kitchen counter, and saw the image of my innocent doe-eyed teenage daughter, holding her backpack. She was silently standing behind me observing the whole terrifying interaction. This was her last summer before she went to college. She suggested maybe there was a logical solution and consoled, "Maybe the screen saver accidentally was moved into a random mode. That could happen. Did you update software lately? It's not definitely a bad guy. You don't have to be afraid."

"With all the cyber chaos around here, there was nothing random about this at all. It was maliciously planned, highly orchestrated and thoughtfully executed. And I'm terrified. Keep all the doors locked," I snapped back in one of those 'I'm the mother so do what I say' tones. I didn't mean to be short with her. I love her.

"God has reasons. He's testing you. Like Job was tested by Satan to see if he was loyal to God. He took away his home and his family and his riches, but all that he lost he got back because he had faith. Anytime anything bad happens, you have to remember God is the redeemer," her innocent voice cajoled.

"You are such a sweet, pure soul," I acknowledged.

"You always tell us that everything happens for a reason. Surely there is a reason for this bad guy in your life. Maybe you are supposed to help him," she said.

If I told my daughter what I was truly thinking of humanity at the time, it would be like I had the decorated tree up and all the stockings stuffed and would in that moment tell her Santa wasn't real. I chose to let her tenderhearted innocence live.

Problems always seem bigger when they are our own, and more solvable from afar. My daughter needed to be far away now, especially with her trusting nature. As much as I selfishly needed her tender solace, I had to protect her from potential harm of any kind.

I sadly advised her, "I love you so much, but it would be best for you to sleep at your dad's house until I resolve my technical issues with the computers. I'll take you out to dinner and take you shopping, but I don't want you here in the house and definitely don't want you to sleep here alone, especially because I'm traveling so much."

Rick and Sick were ruining my life. Now they had the mama-lion syndrome shooting my adrenaline to the sky. One child moved to safety, another lion cub to go. Roar.

My son came home from college that weekend. I took him to dinner at our favorite Park Ave. sidewalk café where he had ordered off the children's menu twice weekly during his childhood. The cool breezes following the daily Florida afternoon rains blew the paper menus, and my hair, which I put into a ponytail to keep out of my face. The winds would catch and whip down the 125-year-old brick streets lined with two story buildings with awnings and historic architectural accents of our little European-style village town center. Winter Park was a safe place to raise children where they could play in the streets and bike to friends' houses. The small city was full of culture and community. It had plein air artists, live street musicians, and well attended Christmas and St. Patty's Day parades full of Girl Scout troops. There was a serenity over dinner in the place I loved and with one of the people I loved more than anyone else on earth.

Dinnertime was sacred in our family as a time to connect and share. Even in public we would whisper a private quick blessing before meals, "Thank you God." My children had impeccable manners. This moment felt normal and peaceful. I ordered my usual grilled salmon with the sweet potato soufflé and sautéed spinach and a Sonoma Cutrer. My son ordered a cheeseburger with fries.

"When you are with me, why don't you order something healthier? You can get cheeseburgers at college," I remarked to the six-foot-three-inch man across from me.

"This is much better than the Big Macs I get at college," he responded with a grin.

"Don't tell me things like that! Do you need more cash to get more nutritious meals? Take care of yourself," I pleaded as the protective mother.

"Also, as part of taking care of yourself, I need you to be very careful of any correspondence you have with me online. Basically, I won't communicate with you online, so if you get something from me, don't open it," I advised, breaking the gentle re-connection with my son like a sledgehammer hitting a Tiffany window.

"OK, what's up? You won't talk to me on the phone, you practically hang up on me, and now no online communication. What's going on? I haven't talked to you in a month," he asked, confused and agitated.

"Well, you know I'm also not inclined towards anything scary or mysterious. I don't like sci-fi anything. You know how you wouldn't even let me watch the TV commercials for scary movies. You'd change the channel or turn off the TV if I was around and a scary movie was being promoted. I'm not a TV watcher at all but it was always on with you guys around. The few scary movies I've seen in my life still have scenes that haunt me like *Jagged Edge*, *Exorcist*, *Magic*, and *Fatal Attraction*. You know, my friends made me see *E.T.*; I thought it might be scary so I didn't want to watch it," I laid the groundwork for the spyware story.

"You are afraid of everything," he laughed.

Then I laid out the details summarizing with, "So, the irony is how I have avoided fright my entire life and I find myself in a mysterious tale of terror."

"I'm really sorry you are scared and that this is happening to you. I don't mean to downplay the fear, but if you weren't my mom, this would be a great thriller film that someone my age would like to see. I can see all of my fraternity brothers wanting to see the film," he suggested.

"Interestingly, I told the same story line to your sister and she saw it as a Bible story and you see it as a screenplay for a horror flick," I noted the difference in my very opposite two children.

"She needs to watch the preach-talk at college. It will be a turn off with the other kids," he said.

"I personally can't remember the time I cared what anyone thought of me. Maybe it was at your age," I said.

"Also, there's an appropriate time to talk of God, especially with a crisis, and certainly in the safety and privacy of our family. In our society, spirituality has a big PR problem. Look at the Facebook boycotts of Chick-fil-A over a religious opinion. In the same week, a psycho mass killer points and shoots guns around and the survivors all have the words 'God' and 'pray' in their sound bites on TV news. On Broadway, when I was growing up, we watched *Jesus Christ Superstar* and then *Joseph and the Amazing Technicolor Dreamcoat*. Now we see *Book of Mormon*. So, God is valuable in our world now for crisis or comedy, right?" I inquired.

"I didn't say I didn't love God. I said that if you talk about it too much, people tune you out. It has the opposite effect. I think religion or spirituality is between individuals and God. It doesn't have to be talked about all the time," he clarified.

"I understand the college cool guy thing but do watch your words. Words have power. Remember who you are. Your family helped found, lead and protect this country just a few hundred years ago for religious freedom," I said.

"Do you remember 911?" I asked him.

"Yes, it was the first time I saw you cry, when the National Anthem started the Gator game on TV," he said.

"Right. Think about that. You were ten-years-old and it was the first tears your mother shed in front of you. You still remember the tears, so remember the passion that caused them. I felt so lucky to return from my Italy trip; I wasn't sure I would be able to. I love you. I love America. I love our freedoms," I reminded him.

"I don't really understand," he confessed, "I don't see how we can lose our national freedoms from spyware on your phone. I know you are upset, but are you overreacting?"

"We are a nation of many people with many phones. We are all connected. What happens to one among us, happens to all of us. If you allow a little evil, much evil will follow. Think about this, at your age, your grandfather left his college football scholarship to fight in World War Two. His plane got shot down over France and he spent two years in a Nazi prisoner of war camp. He easily could have died several times over protecting the America that he loved. What is it within you that you would be willing to fight for? What would you die for to protect? What do you cherish? What do you treasure?" I asked.

As we paid the bill with cash, and then walked under the stars towards our cars, I had my son wish on the first star of the evening.

"Do you remember when you were little I would have you tell me what you wished for?" I asked.

"Yes, you aren't supposed to tell anyone your wishes," he laughed.

"And, that is how I made sure your wishes came true as best as I could in your childhood," I chuckled back.

Humor cures. We laughed a lot when we were together. I wanted to end our dinner on a high note. I didn't like sharing this *Saturday Night Live* Debbie Downer side with my children.

From the open-air bistro across the street we could hear the acoustic guitar and solo vocalist singing a Dave Matthews song, "Where are you going with your long face pulling down ..."

My son was going back to summer school. I was going crazy. I wanted to be going in the direction of my lifetime goals and dreams. I didn't choose this path. The path chose me.

CHAPTER 15, LAST SUMMER RESEARCH ON HACKERS

Still on the boat, trolling along, reclining with my eyes closed, I continued to daydream about the details of last summer.

Another desperate call during the trauma, was to a guy who had helped me with code on a website once. He lived for Macs. He was obsessed by Macs. Mac counter-Attack! He'd be the guy to help. I nicknamed him Mack, his real name was Mark.

Mack told me, "If you handed your iPhone to a technically oriented guy who wanted to stalk you, it's all over with."

He continued, "Everything he would need to clone your phone so he could listen or participate anytime is in your AT&T account page on your iPhone. He could create and IMEI sim chip and plug it into another phone and listen all day. If he had access to your Mac, and it sounds like the iMac was vulnerable at your office, then he could have set up key logging where another computer duplicates whatever you are creating on your Mac. You can put up a firewall but if you lose your data, there's no way to get it back. Get rid of the Windows XO old PC; there's no way to have security with it so shut it down. Back up everything private on a thumb drive, which then you might lose. There's not a clear cut answer and the technology changes literally daily; even I can't keep up with it."

He pulled out his iPhone from his pocket to show me the screen, and continued, "Facebook and other social media are easy entries into your data. Set up all the safety features and change your passwords often. You think the young women are the easy prey on social media, but in reality, they grew up with technology so are more savvy than you moms. Do you have a password on Facebook? When was the last time you changed it? Do you have all the safety features on?"

"Show me the safety features. I already turned off the GPS feature. Logically, I post my travels and events a week or so later. I don't want someone breaking into my home or my condo when I am at the other location, or somewhere else. I post news but never too personal and never in real time," I said.

"Look, if a guy wants to hack back in, he will get back in. Guys like that practice all the time for fun at Starbucks and public Wi-Fi spaces. Those places are petri dishes of computer viruses. Guys sit around and grab whatever bit of data they can. They grab any bit of information. Never do online banking or credit card tasks in public. If you make those places your virtual office, you'll pick up more creeps. Also, be really careful when you log into Wi-Fi sites because they might be decoy sites that look like the legitimate log in site. Look, don't feel bad. It's not just you getting victimized. Cyber crime is in the billions and quickly surpassing drugs as the global crime cash cow," Mack said.

He continued in a more intense mode. He leaned towards me and lowered his voice, "Serious hackers do black box events which are secret online events. Hackers play games and at a specified time, with specified rules, hack into people, places and things. It's a whole underground culture. You can't fight it. It's like a vampire, invisible and bloodthirsty. The corporate world plays into it. I got hired at Lockheed when they tracked me down after I hacked into them for fun. They wanted me on their side to keep guys like me out of their systems that might be hacking for harm, not just for a challenge. There are actually hacking companies that big corporations hire to show them their weak security links."

"This isn't comforting," I whined, "All I heard from you is clone, key logging, and can't keep him or them out!"

"Accept it as our world today and just try to protect your data as best as you can and move on with your life," Mack shrugged.

He gave lots of advice about backing up data, which I tuned out. I'm good about keeping a digital and printed copy of anything of importance. One of my clients asked me jokingly one time, "Do you have something against trees?" My family had owned a big timber business so actually I love trees, but paper is my preference for documenting life.

I interjected to Mack, "I'm good about backing up. The tricky part is keeping it all filed and labeled so you can find data again. I worked on a marketing plan for an offsite data storage company right before 911. With that tragedy bringing to light the great need for the service, the company took off and they hired a large ad agency. In the process of their marketing plan work, I learned about data back up. I keep a dedicated external drive on each computer. I check the backups regularly, and also back up by burning CDs, which I save offsite in a safety deposit box. I like the CDs because they are easy to label with a Sharpie. Not all computers have CD readers now and flash drives are smaller and hold more data. I back up on both. With continual new technology, for anything really important, I have to remember to format the data so it can be read by new software or hardware. Backing up by itself isn't enough over the years. I wonder now if my automated external hard drive La-cie backup is embedding all these issues right along with my data. Maybe? Probably?"

When Mack left, I changed my password on my Gmail account to "G@dProtectMe1111" and Google rated the strength "strong" for long, upper/lower characters, numbers and characters. "Yes, strong," I agreed to myself.

Do one thing at a time until the issue is fixed.

As I was changing my password, the doorbell startled me. Normal sounds like a doorbell, an oak tree branch landing on my roof, a cat meowing outside, all could shock me and set off a panic attack. My friend Ben was delivering a book I was going to review for him. He joined me for a glass of wine and a listen to my sad saga. Ben's ad-vice I always took from his worldly perspective and also his intuitive sense, which was quite strong. Ben was one of my favorite people to mentor me on two of my favorite topics, writing and spirituality.

"You are in danger! This guy is wacko, dangerous, no reality. You are on a webcam. He plans to post sex scenes of you. My son was of the era that he was into techie geek games. The smart ones got bored with video games and a real person to target is a game to them. They grew up with emotionless and lifeless keyboards and monitors, not hide-n-seek and cowboys-and-Indians like we did. They didn't touch humans in games of tag. Cartoons don't cry when you hurt them so these kids just don't understand. Then they grow up. They don't relate to people well. They don't even hear you or your cries because they fried their eardrums with loud music and sounds funneled through headphones. They know no boundaries. It's a power trip. This guy following you doesn't think he has to follow the law. He'll stay a step ahead of you, so you can't catch him at his own game. You have to tell him you already have the proof and are going to get legal authorities involved. Tell him you will ruin his career. You have to cripple him before he infects others. He's looney, obsessed, and has time to devote to stalking you. You have to save yourself, then you have to teach people how to protect themselves. You have to write about him. It's like you break your leg and learn to walk again, then you teach other people how to heal and walk again," he warned.

We finished our wine and whine. When he left, I turned on every light in the house and turned the motion detector alarm on. I turned on *I Love Lucy* on Nickelodeon and wished Rick and Sick would vanish and Ricky Ricardo would come in to save me from my own sticky, zany, crazy calamity.

Owen's CIA guy got me in to his office that next afternoon. I pulled up to a sea of General Motors mid-sized gray cars, obviously government issued, with a lot of smart nerdy looking men in a lot of brown suits.

The CIA guy I met with was handsome, gregarious and helpful. He didn't look like the brown suited spy guys downstairs. He was capable and straightforward and got right down to business. He hooked my Mac up to his and their mainframe for diagnostics and gave two hours of advice. Key word is Mac. He had two Macs on his desk. He could speak my language.

He gave this advice, "I suggest you wipe these devices and / or buy new ones. It's very possible it's all compromised. Mac just had their first major virus. The hackers ignored Mac for a long time because the Apple sales numbers were lower than PCs. Now with the popularity of iPhones and iPads, they are vulnerable for recreational hackers out to create mayhem as a game. Run anti-virus software such as Norton, although some computer people think the Norton itself becomes virus-like and bogs down speed. Be wary of anyone near your devices installing video cameras with a remote view. It's rampant. Download all of your updates weekly. The software companies and Apple itself update with virus protection. We can contact the FBI, but with cyber crime, you'll have to show $10,000 to $20,000 in damages minimum to get the local police involved first and it's nearly impossible to prove. You need to file a report immediately about the one guy as an incident for your physical safety in case he is dangerous. Change your passwords regularly using

14-character alpha-numeric with special characters. With an eight-character password, a rainbow bot cracks it immediately. Disable guest accounts. Ninety percent of hackers infilterate through social engineering, like what happened to you, such as borrowing a phone. Don't let anyone borrow your phone!"

He unhooked my Mac from his diagnostic program running on his Mac, turned it off, and handed it to me, shaking his head from side to side.

He could have had my answers and solutions, but he told me he didn't have the time to help me, and I didn't have enough money to pay him to help me. He said most major companies, institutions, or entities, don't have enough resources to entirely stop hacking. I wasn't alone. Boy, I sure felt alone.

I left the CIA compound and drove to the local police station. I took my handwritten and photocopied documents to file an incident report so if I made the 911 call, they would have a record at the station.

The policeman listened to my elevator speech version of the chaos, which I had perfected by now, "A creepy guy put spyware on my phone and computers. I'm not sure why and I'm not sure if he'll hurt me but I am scared and I want it to stop and I want him in jail. I don't know how to document it but I'm working on that. He's ruining my life. Can you help me?"

"Did you date him?" he asked.

"Everyone asks that! If I had dated the guy, which I did not, would it then be acceptable and legal for him to stalk me and torture me? No I didn't date him, he's just some sketchy guy I barely know," I responded, miffed.

"You have to fill out your report on our form," said the officer on duty. He was short, stocky, physically fit and talked with a Southern drawl. He had short-cropped sandy blonde hair that receded making a perfect line through the top of his head. He was the classic bubba-type I had grown up with in Old Florida. I wouldn't want to be a fleeing criminal fighting this guy's speed, strength or ability to accurately hit a moving target with a bullet.

The form was taking too long to fill out and it was emotional sitting in this cave-like, stark, locked institutional building.

He was chatty and kept me company as I filled in his form, "These guys are cyber cowards. They prey upon women then spread their terror ideas for copycats. They can be very hard to catch if you know them. If you have no connection to them and their motive is paying back society with revenge and anger and rage, it can be nearly impossible. They do criminal abusive acts behind the veil of keystrokes and subversive software. With the internet, a stranger a world away can find you online in normal life and wipe normal from your vocabulary," he chatted.

"On this gorgeous sunny day, I feel like I am the persecuted one locked up and in jail instead of me being the victim. I'll fill it out and bring it back. Thanks for your help," I told him.

"On your papers, be sure to use the words 'industrial sabotage' so it's a criminal offense and note that this is an incident report that you are gathering further information to upgrade to a criminal offense," he advised.

The officer held open the heavy door for me and walked outside into the parking lot with me.

"So, did you grow up around here?" he asked.

"Yes," I responded aware that he had walked me out so he could talk outside of the recorded walls of the police station.

"These cowards need a lesson. You aren't the first person in here complaining about these wimps. You know who the guy is. Don't you know a man who can give him a lesson in manners?" he asked, and gestured a fist punching the palm of his other hand.

"Every man's man I've told so far has that same suggestion. I haven't totally ruled it out yet. I'd prefer to handle it correctly and give a step by step easy to follow solution for other people if this happens to them. That is my perfect world. A peaceful solution and back to my peaceful life," I shared and gave him a big hug. I liked the feeling of the big loaded pistol against my hip, not in a sexual way, but in a primal survival way.

Owen had offered to bring me over a Smith and Wesson pistol. I've had them in the house before but would get rid of them because I lived with children. Now I live by myself and now I also live with the S&W he offered me. It sits with the bullets loaded, unlocked by my bed. You aren't supposed to keep loaded guns around;

Guns 101 rule. A bad guy breaks a rule, then a good guy breaks a rule, then it's the Wild West. I grew up with *Gunsmoke* in the background on TV even though, again, I'm not much of a TV watcher. I take my son occasionally to the shooting range; every man should be able to handle a gun. I'm a tomboy who grew up visiting the Deep South male cousins who were always astonished at how good of a shot I was at Coke cans and at sporting clays. I didn't really like to kill the birds, and the small animals. I really couldn't kill the living animals. Inanimate objects, bullseye. No problem. Bad guy in my own home. Hope it never happens. But, well, No problem.

While a Smith and Wesson is right on target for the physical world, Molly my spiritual advisor gave me ammunition for predicting Rick's game last summer. I saw her once a year, like a doctor's checkup, for an hour of advice. I looked at it like an hour of entertainment such as viewing a soap opera. I didn't guide my life by her advice, or anybody's advice, but rather looked for an affirmation or direction. I was astonished at how much information she could provide in such a short time, and even more amazed at how accurate she was.

Since my post divorce self discovery phase, I had seen a dozen spiritual advisors in several countries. I tested them, and they all told me the same consistent overall story of my life. The pivotal crossroads were to happen at this point in my life, and, look! Here they are! I had always been intuitive. I didn't have a label for it until I started researching spirituality after my divorce. I had always been religious, which gave a framework of knowledge to allow spirituality make sense.

The advice and input from Molly didn't always make sense at the time, but if I took notes and read it a few months later, it would sometimes be right on target. I might initially misread the person or details she was speaking of, but in time, I would understand her seemingly confusing messages.

On the topic of my current cyber challenge, she wasn't confused, but very clear. Molly saw Rick right away and warned, "Polarizing powers of the universe are in play. This man is strongly drawn to you, to your light. He doesn't even know why. He is entirely unaware, but he is, in fact, aligned with darkness. You will overcome him, but not without a battle. You have been prepared for this."

A blue jay landed on the windowsill of her historic Victorian home. I tuned out for a minute. I'd like to tune out and ignore the whole reality. I'd like to fly away like a little bird, but the drama was continuing when I mentally tuned back in.

"He'd like to be a couple with you. His life is upside down. He's confused. Be careful. Be afraid. He's dangerous. The guy is a stalker and knows all about you. You'll get rid of him. Men will help you. He's a vengeful coward. His energy field is bad. You aren't very fun to be around with this troubled man in your life. Get rid of him. Be strong. Write the book about it by hand and you'll have to input it on a friend's computer. Go to the police. They will get him," she reported.

"I'm glad to hear this will have closure. It feels now like it might just continue forever," I responded in great relief.

"I've never told anyone about this recurring vision I've had my whole life, but I am concerned that it's related to this challenge I'm having now," I said.

"You are quite intuitive yourself. If you sense it's related, it is," said Molly.

"The short version of the vision is this, it starts at the end of Worth Ave. in Palm Beach. I didn't know that was the place until the first time I visited there. I had chills and was momentarily paralyzed at the first sighting of it. Overlooking this gorgeous pristine beach, out of the blue, in the distance on the horizon, I see a mammoth tidal wave building and rushing towards the shore. Just as the wall of water hits shore, the brilliant colors fade to monochrome and all turns to slow motion. The vision becomes fuzzy like viewing through a steamy shower door. The deafening thunder of the tidal wave grows louder till it hits land, then everything becomes totally silent. In my dream, I can fly, so I fly maybe 30-feet above ground, up and down streets, over all the places in Florida that I've ever lived or visted. The scenes click like watching a slide show from community to community. I look down and see the screams on the faces of the people as they run randomly from building to building, looking all around in confusion and intense terror. In slow motion, the giant wave washes through the buildings and down the streets. It's not really water, but more of a clear vaporous wave. It's hard to describe," I said.

"Above the clouds, another thunderous noise presents the hooves of massive war horses in full armor. The beasts emerge climbing from a single foxhole in the clouds. From the hole, the warriors of the ages, dressed in full battle gear, sprint up and run in all directions as far as the eye can see. The thickness of the multitudes of pairs and small groups of warriors, from antiquity to current day, fill the horizon in a perfect circle. Native Americans wear war paint and have bows drawn. World War II men have purple hearts and pistols. Ancient Vikings, Romans, Mongols, African tribesmen, and the mighty eras of every nation are collected in the armor of their day," I closed my eyes and tried to describe.

"Here's the really scary part. The black and white vision ends each time, when I look up and see a 30-foot-tall half of a face of a man with dark clouds and fire behind him. He's in big neon colors. His piercing eyes are delighting in the pandemonium and then he fixes his sights on me flying by myself above the mess. The fright wakes me each time. It feels like I meet the essence of evil face-to-face. I've had this vision all of my life and parts of it almost daily now. Does it have anything to do with this spyware stuff?" I asked.

Molly was normally animated. Molly was normally talking and I was listening. Molly was poker-faced and hesitated for a moment.

"The people are silenced right?" she asked and didn't wait for a response and said, "It could be related to cyber security and communication. This is for you to understand. I don't have your answer."

Molly went back to Rick, "Start with what you can control. He's stalking others, too, and they are tolerating his bad behavior. He's a real pervert and some of the women are embarrassed to stand up to him."

She told me some things about my love life and career that I didn't remember. The report on Rick made my skin crawl so I recall it like it was yesterday.

Leaving Molly's office, I "got" that some of the women he encountered might be embarrassed because they had kinky sex with him. The night of the spyware incident with Rick, he insisted on meeting me in the parking lot and walking into Buccan with me. Right there on South County Road in Palm Beach, right across from the police department, Rick brazenly unbuttoned his shirt and proudly showed me a brutally bruised chest, stomach and arms.

"Oh, my God! What happened to you? Put your shirt back on," I shrieked.

"I had rough sex last night. Everyone is doing it," he reported like a Cheshire cat with a big ear to ear grin.

"That's sick. I don't want to know about your sex life and certainly not about that kinky stuff," I told him.

"I thought we were friends?" he asked.

"Not that kind of friends. You keep your private life to yourself and I'll keep mine to myself, OK?" I demanded.

We walked in the restaurant to meet a group of friends. Within two hours of that conversation, we wouldn't be friends, and my sex life, or any part of my life for that matter, wouldn't be private from him. It dawned on me later that he was showing off and his ego was bruised along with his flesh, that I wasn't impressed by his show of sexual bravado.

I didn't believe at the time that normal women would do that to a man having fun sex unless she was in harm's way. Out of concern, I called the Palm Beach police the next day to see if anyone reported a rape or a missing person. It was creepy. He was creepy. Thankfully there were no reports.

I later related my friend Ben telling me, "These guys get off on the adrenaline of cyber stalking. They get sexual arousal from viewing and hearing the unobtainable on screen rather than the scent of pheromones or the tickle of a teasing touch. They've spent more time with video games than flirting games with girls. They don't even know how to be in love or make love. Most of them prefer S & M and bondage as part of the whole misfit perception of relationships. Lots of these guys are money guys, too. Tech guys pull in cash and dole it out, so some women indulge them and the cycle perpetuates itself."

Spiritual counselor Molly confirmed the imminent danger. There wasn't much comfort in having my worst fears confirmed, so I visited my psychologist counselor, Jill, the next day. I didn't see Jill often; generally once or twice with a boyfriend breakup and a time or two for teenage children concerns and questions. Like most of my inner circle, she was aware and intuitive. She gave practical advice and rapid solutions. I either hadn't had major problems so far in life, or Jill was exceptionally talented. Either way I needed an hour with her. With all the crazy happenings on my computers, I had to make sure I stayed sane.

I already knew what I would tell Jill, along with more of the details of the stalking, so she'd understand why I felt paranoid, concerned and depressed. I wanted to make the most of my one hour with her so I said it aloud in the car driving to her office, "I'm just not myself. I'm not sleeping. I can't work and I love my work. I'm terrified. I go into the Apple Store for help and I think people are following me in the parking lot. I drive around my block two or three times before I pull into my garage to see if anyone is parked outside. I whisper talking to my daughter in my own home so 'the phone' won't hear me. It's awful. I have self-diagnosed myself with a mild case of depression. I can't go on this way. Please help me keep my mental stability until I can get this insane creep out of my life."

I gave Jill a hug and walked in and sat on the comfy overstuffed sofa in the back corner office in the quiet church compound. She gave me a concerned gaze and asked, "So, are you OK?"

"Well, no, not at all. You see, in the last two months, I've had this creepy stalker guy all in my business and he's ruining my life," I blurted out and grabbed a tissue from the box on the mahogany table beside me. The soft 15 watt light burned my hand slightly as I scraped against it. Even in the big comfy sofa, I was really awkward and uncomfortable. I was mad. No, not mad, I was pissed beyond belief that here I was in the middle of a workday, spending my precious time and my hard earned money getting counseling for mental anguish I never asked for.

To my great astonishment, Jill's response was, "I know you are going through a tough time. Breakups are hard. Thank you for referring Rick to me. He was in here yesterday and started telling me his side of your troubles."

I'm not much of a screamer, but I totally lost it and screamed, "What? What? What? He was in here getting counseling? There is no combined 'your' troubles. He is the definition of trouble. Oh my God! He is a total pathological liar. He is a stalker. He is a pervert. You have no idea who was just in here."

"He seemed a little off but understandably because he is upset. So, let's talk about you and how you are feeling about all of this," she said.

"Jill, listen, he's spying on me and listening to all my calls so he heard me making this appointment. He's reading all my e-mails so he saw your confirmation e-mail and that is how he got your phone number to call you. I didn't give him your number. I haven't talked to him in over a month. I never want to talk to him again. I want him to go away, far away. And, very important for you to understand, I never dated him. It's in his imagination that it was even remotely possible for us to date. You've met my boyfriends, Jill, he's not my type. And, for starters, he is crazy," I tried to jolt sense into her.

I wasn't sure if she believed me. She was looking at me like I was the fantasy-crazed deranged person. No, I have a stalker and I am the victim. I explained more of the details, now wasting most of the hour defending that I hadn't dated him, more than the psychological torture I was enduring. Frankly, this was just more torture of fire on open wounds.

"It must be terrible for someone who has been successful to feel so powerless. You have to know this is not your fault. You simply befriended a bad person and loaned him your phone. It could have happened to me, or anyone. I agree with you that you'll have to fix your security issues before we can fix your mental state. Your emotional state is understandable with the stress you are under," Jill said.

I left not knowing if she believed me. I wasn't sure what she was referring to about my mental state. I'm not sure we even talked about me. The session wasn't very healing. Her weak validation wasn't any more comforting than Molly's stringent advice. I wanted an ambulance and I wasn't even getting Band-Aids. Both Molly and Jill confirmed basically, "Your life sucks now and there's not much you can do about it."

I sat on the bench in the courtyard for a few minutes and put on my Chanel sunglasses with the bow on the sides. I was in my usual girly sundress and strappy sandals. I didn't feel girly. I felt like I was being forced to be a man. Aren't men supposed to protect women? Nobody was protecting me. Nothing was as it was supposed to be. Everything was shifting and in motion. And now, Rick was brazenly crashing into my inner circle. I sat shaking for a few minutes and tried to feign a cheerful hello to the people walking by on the sidewalk. I couldn't move. I was totally frozen in fear. The reality was that Rick was in this very parking lot yesterday. He might still be in Winter Park today. I couldn't move. I looked, and looked, and looked at the parking lot to see if I saw him hiding in or around or behind any of the cars. I finally mustered the courage to put one foot in front of the other. I pulled off my heels and ran barefoot to my car, locked the doors, and sped away towards home.

Home was a concept that now posed double trouble, since I had my home and my rental condo three hours away. Clearly there was no way for me to protect myself, my family, and my belongings in two separate venues. I called Captain and gave him the Palm Beach condo key and had him bring to my Winter Park home anything that looked personal. I showed him photos and pointed out the items that were mine. He might not get them all. It didn't matter. I e-mailed the Realtor and gave my 30-day notice and mailed the final check.

On this topic of the Palm Beach condo, I really had wanted to ask Jill's advice about a bridge I burned, another casualty of the spy fiasco. A very meticulous friend wanted to schedule time at the condo and was sending me all these fact-filled details of her plans to visit there. I tried to explain to her to stop sending the e-mails and I told her it was for safety reasons. I told her to only communicate with me directly in person about her travel plans. She couldn't help her detailed-self and kept sending the e-mails. For her safety, I gave her a generic excuse that it wasn't convenient for her to visit there. The real truth was that I wouldn't even be there but I didn't want her there for her own sake.

A few weeks later, in the mail I got a handwritten letter explaining that she didn't think I was a very good friend and she didn't want to spend time with me. At least she finally listened and didn't e-mail the letter. I put on my to-do list to communicate with this girl that I was trying to save her from being victimized by a stalker who was already casing the condo. I was by definition being a friend, even if she didn't think so. My to-do list of making up to people, starting with my children, this girl, my clients, my friends I hadn't seen in weeks, was growing by the hour. I was the victim and yet it seemed I owed apologies to everyone for my out-of-character behavior. I wondered how many people I might have offended during this extreme self-protective state, that I didn't even realize.

The boat ride was lingering and long. I grabbed a beach towel from under the seat, and moved to the front of the boat to take a cat nap. I hummed to myself the Riteous Brothers tune *Unchained Melody*, "Loney rivers flow to the sea, to the sea, To the open arms of the sea..." I was thinking of my boyfriend as we boated along.

Long distance boyfriends are the best and Ted was the love of my life, this part of my life anyway. He loved his boat named Sunny. He loved boating in Marsh Harbor and all around the Bahamas and Florida. He loved fine dining, like at the famous Wally's where I would meet him when we got to the marina. Most importantly, he loved me. He was a great listener and super supportive.

His family made their money from an investment in tanning salon equipment and they had sold the company. Now Ted works as a wealth manager, mostly his own wealth. You meet a lot of guys in South Florida who claim similar pasts. Ted's happens to be true. The company engineered and manufactured World War II guns then car parts. They sold when his dad got sick in 1990, so Ted was flush. He lived in Las Olas on the canal so he could get Sunny, his go-fast high performance Contender boat, out for frequent fishing excursions. He had two grown children. He was divorced once like me. He was good to his mother. I believe you can tell how a man will treat the woman in his life by how he treats his mother. Ted worked still. He managed a few other client's funds and kept an office in Ft. Lauderdale. He mostly worked from his laptop and iPhone like me, so we met all over the country, and all over the world. We would sometimes travel with just each other, sometimes to meet with his clients, and sometimes to meet Owen for fishing or for business. Owen and Ted had become friends and had partnered in a few business ventures. Ted was funny, smart, and sexy. He was a fisherman and a foodie. Shirtless, he could cleat hitch a yacht in a boat slip, and just as easily slip on a bow-tie for a fundraiser at Mar-a-lago, Trump's estate on Palm Beach island. We could have fun at sunrise on a deserted island beach in wet swimsuits, and he'd be just as fun suited up watching sunset at The Top of The Standard in New York.

I met him on a girls' getaway with Ann in Key West. He was on a guys fishing trip. He looked much like the rest of the room full of tan, salty, hot, athletic, 50-something men. He had business-man brown short straight hair with gray specs on the sides, and big brown eyes. He had a tenor voice and could mimic Tim McGraw after a few cocktails. He knew the words to every country song. Nothing about him was country, or Southern, but he said he liked the earthy lyrics of the music. We were both word people.

His first words to me were not so original, "Don't I know you from somewhere?"

I retorted with a line borrowed from a wilder friend, recently divorced, "I'm not sure. I'm looking for a man with a Harley, a man with a tattoo, and a man strong enough to make love to me while holding me up against a wall."

I didn't really want the Harley guy or the tattoo guy. Ted flexed his biceps and pecks and proudly exclaimed, "I'm your number three man!"

His guy pack was having a girl-hunting contest that night to see who could scare up dinner dates the quickest. Ted didn't win the quickest that contest, but the longest date, some seven years now. We met on the first night at the iconic Hemmingway's bar over mojitos, met up every day for dinner that week, and have continued dating long distance.

First impressions count and Ted was an aim-to-please can-do kinda' guy. After our time apart, we'd generally start our sequence of sexual encounters with a steamy shower with soapy steamier sex, up against the wall, just as ordered on day one. The first few times, I worried about us slipping and needing a naked ambulance ride for stitches or broken bones. Somehow with the motion, he would find the correct angle where we wouldn't fall. We'd suds each other sufficiently to tease and taunt and tingle. He'd grab me, push me up against the slippery tile wall, and then the passion would play out with the mutual screams echoed and magnified in the small wet space of a shower.

Last summer, during the turmoil, Ted was a welcome diversion from the cyber chaos. I felt safe in his presence and invincible in his arms. Ted is a man's man and would protect his woman, and himself, with vigor. He's strong, honorable, compassionate, and direct. He is the living definition of "meek," which is "strength under control." I heard that in a sermon once and knew it would be the defining characteristic of my man. Ted is meek. You can trust the guy. I trust him whole-heartedly as we both move around the world separated, to come back together when we can in our travels.

With my cyber situation igniting fear, anger, suspicion, paranoia, distrust, desperation and animal-instinct survivalism, I found myself setting subtle booby traps for Ted even, the person I trusted more than anyone in the whole world. Family, friends, co-workers, neighbors, any one of them could have collaborated with the enemy in covert deception to help create my hell. Maybe a neighbor agreed to let a creep park a car at their house that housed the guy who sat there till he cracked my modem code. The person who got into my PC through the Wi-Fi modem maybe was a person and not a computer bot. Maybe a client or freelancer e-mailed an infected file to me. Maybe that pain-in-the-butt assistant, who complained all the time, let my competitor into the office to install spyware on the iMac she used. Maybe one of my Palm Beach friends was checking up on me so she could report my strategy and progress to Rick. Maybe Ted had something to do with the nightmare. Nobody had access to my home, my Macs, my phone, my passwords, my life itself more than Ted. I trusted him but I still found myself on those summer visits, placing a piece of mail perfectly perpendicular on my day-timer that I still used some, or on the closed Mac laptop to see if it moved one centimeter. I found myself waking at night, since I could barely sleep anyway, and intently listening if he walked into the kitchen for a water bottle. I found myself questioning if he really needed a key to my house and to my car. I changed my home alarm code and didn't tell Ted or my children the new code; I told them to let me know if they were coming by and when. None of this paranoid behavior resembled the happy-go-lucky skipping-around-the-globe writer of all-good-things person I was before spyware entered my life.

Last June during the crazy era, Ted and I met in Naples at the Cove Inn by the Naples city docks where he docked his Contender Sunny. The funky fifties motif rentable condos were the perfect launch spot for the Naples Fifth Avenue and Third Street restaurants, including our favorite, Campiello's. Ted preferred the Atlantic coast, but we visited Naples on the Gulf of Mexico once or twice a year for variety, generally after a Florida Keys trip.

We lit mango-scented candles in honor of my all-time favorite book, *Seventeen Ways To Eat A Mango*, about a fruit canning executive who went to an island to expand his business and decided to stay on the island. I'm an executive and a capitalist, but I started as a surf chick. A beach bag of swimsuits, a boat, and an island bar and I'm good for a while.

We poured some Sonoma Cutrer Chardonnay, put our Cuddle Country Pandora station on that we created with our favorite tunes, danced in the moonlit room, and seduced each other. He gently grabbed my waist from behind and pulled himself close to me, kissing the back of my neck. He took my brush and brushed my hair. Ted was a breast guy. He caressed starting with my breasts, and admired my body in whole, in the reflection of the mirror.

"You are the most beautiful woman in the world. You are all good things: beautiful on the inside and out, intelligent, loving, sexy. I love you. Only you. I want you. I need you. I just want to eat you. I wish I could crawl inside you and never be separate from you. You are the love of my life. You are my soul mate," he whispered in my ear.

As much as I loved the physical part of seduction, I am a word person, and nobody could sing me to shivers like Ted could. His voice was a seductress to me. I melted into him.

I like the words. He's a guy. He likes the physical part. The clothes all slipped off both of us within two songs. We slipped into the shower. Sex never lasted too long in the shower because we had shower sex when we were re-uniting after having been apart for maybe a few days, maybe a week or two. The first sessions come quickly.

We were drying off and preparing for dinner. Pandora stopped. We had brought the music into the room with us like we always did. But we didn't always have a stalker. I didn't even think about it in the moment. Now there was this moment. We had a cyber threesome.

The music stopped playing and the Mac was silent. The screen

77

saver was flashing stock photography of master artworks featuring nudes. Our cyber curator flashed us mostly Tahitian Gauguin paintings. We looked aghast in anticipation of doom at each other and moved closer to the Mac.

Sending both of us back a few feet in fright, the Mac blared out Phantom of the Opera's *Music of the Night* starting mid-song with the lyrics, "Touch me, trust me, savor each sensation, Let the dream begin, let your darker side give in..."

We tried to turn off the Mac and stop the maddening music, and when we would approach the keys, the nudes would flash rapidly startling us. The volume increased and the song played itself twice then sat silent. We sat in shock motionless and speechless.

"The asshole is in here with us now. He probably recorded us," spat Ted.

The music started up again, luring us close to the monitor. Kelly Clarkson's *Dark Side* blared out the lyrics, "Everybody's got a dark side, Do you love me? ..." The slide show before us now was not of classical paintings, but our worst nightmare, of us. Our cyber stalker had video of us today in the shower. That wasn't the worst. He had a whole two-minute-or-so film production of spliced sexual interludes we had experienced in my home.

"How did Rick film that?" screamed Ted.

"I can guess. He probably sat outside the house and hacked into the closed circuit security cameras at the house. All he had to do was hack into the IP address of the CCTV system, and he could see my, and our, every move. I already thought of that with all the advice I've been getting so I already disconnected it if that makes you feel any better," I said trying to calm him down.

"No! I don't feel good about any of this crap," screamed Ted, throwing his arms motioning towards the laptop. Ted snatched up his clothes, and stormed out onto the balcony overlooking the marina, wearing a towel wrapped around his waist.

"I don't feel very good myself," I breathed into the empty room.

Ted had a long fuse. For him to lose his temper took a lot. This was a lot. This was hell. In a way, I was glad he saw first hand how emotional and horrifying the spying was, but I never, ever, ever wanted it to affect Ted. I now felt like Ted was upset with me for bringing the dysfunction into our lives. It must be the way women feel when they are raped, a hopeless and helpless feeling wrapped in shame for being so stupid to let it happen to you. As a victim, you have to overcome the guilt that maybe somehow you weren't diligent or careful enough; that maybe you could have prevented it. Rape, just like this crime, happens to you and then also to everyone you love. It spreads like a cancer with no cure.

Ted and I didn't discuss the sex video incident further then in Naples or ever. We both knew he, they, it, shithead, someone had documented us in a private moment, uh wait, private moments. This evil presence obviously wasn't kind or moral so we waited for a bribery note or some other soap opera drama move, which thankfully didn't come. It was quite possible that the sick mind wanted it only for his own personal twisted pleasure. It was also quite possible that at any moment on any random day in our futures, sick-slick-dickhead could decide to post the thing somewhere. Maybe it's running now with Japanese subtitles. Maybe Ted now has Rick's face Photoshop-ed. How would we know? With real-time world-wide internet, our private moments could be posted most anywhere. That Naples incident was last summer and the freak film hadn't debuted anywhere as far as we could tell in the last year.

CHAPTER 18, MORE SLEUTHING AND SOLUTIONS

The boat was bouncing slightly towards the open horizon. I sipped a Diet Coke and went back into my deep-thought trance of the events that unfolded last summer.

The shared spy activity, from what I could tell by studying for hours upon hours on all the computers, was in Users, Shared, Adobe Alias. When I checked onto my computer, I'd check Recent Items under the Apple menu first. Since I had unplugged the iMac, I had one Mac and it's backup drive frozen in time as evidence.

The Adobe Drive on Mac Pro had a pop up menu that read, "The Adobe Drive allows you to connect to a Version Cue Server just like a regular hard drive. Simply connect the Version Cue Server from the Drive Connection screen and enter your username and password for the service. The service will then appear like another hard drive that you can access from any application."

It was malfunctioning because it was connected to the iMac account "Team" and iMac was now unplugged.

This could explain why I always have a Remote Disc icon, which I can't click on or get rid of. If I burn a CD, two icons pop up. If I print something, two printers pop up on my monitor in unison. I was one. Who for sure was two? And why? This was the work of number two stalker, Mr. Sick.

I continued my sleuthing and solution seeking and little else for several months. My entire life was consumed with getting my privacy, my sense of safety, and my life back. I told one client who had an answer for me: a very capable, very expensive, very available to come to your home or office, very Mac savvy Don.

I had him come by the day I got his number. "Sure, if someone had physical access to your computer, it could be as simple as a program called gotomypc.com. There are lots of programs out there designed for someone like you who wants to access a second computer. You would like the idea if it were you using it and not someone who is scaring you," he said.

"The only other way would be if you didn't have usernames or passwords on your modem or your computer, and you left it on all the time, and you didn't move it for a long time, then it would just be a matter of time before a bot found it. They are searching the internet all the time. They run malware in the background of your computer and you don't even know the bot has come and left malware there," he said.

"Don, yes, yes, and yes. I have been a sitting duck for years. I am textbook dum-dum," I meekly confessed to him that I had all of those conditions.

He continued, "Well, then, entities can access your computer and be running programs in the background which you don't see and don't know are there."

"Is it like spyware on your phone that it would slow down the functions?" I asked.

"Absolutely, depending upon how much is being used by the entity," he said.

"I only use this Dell PC for Quickbooks but I have to wait for up to a minute for it to send one check to the printer. It's got so much memory and RAM because I don't use it for anything but account-ing. Do you think it has issues?" I asked, already sensing the answer.

"PCs have been targeted by hackers for decades since the numbers of PCs are so big. Everyone has one, or two, or three. It's easier for me to do diagnostics on a PC because just like there are more viruses, there are more software solutions to get rid of the viruses on a PC. It's all new to Mac, so they need to develop anti-virus quickly. You have to be careful running Norton on the Mac because some-times it becomes in effect a virus and slows down the functions. All the software solutions need tweaking," he said and bent down over the PC keyboard and clicked on pages of code that seemed to mean something to him.

He scanned up and down the long list of code on the monitor and made a few "hhhhmmmm" sounds then remarked, "You probably have been compromised by a bot. See here is the code buried in the printer font file?"

He pointed to some code on the monitor that meant absolutely nothing to me. It meant something to him, so progress was made.

So, now I have Rick, Sick and Bot, the cyber terror trio. I feel like I've taken my computers to a clinic in the third world for help and only got more viruses and issues and we're all in critical care on life support.

Not much I told him seemed to surprise him or rattle him. He gave answers in a slow precise manner in easy to understand terms like a college professor. He was so hired!

"You opened the malware the guy sent you, so it's like phishing and pharming, where e-mails and websites look legitimate but wreak havoc in your system," he explained.

He pulled up the data activity reports, which were easy to find but I had never seen before with any of my other stream of experts, and started reading the activity recorded within the computer. It listed in computer jargon every single task the computer did in great detail. This is proof. He copied the files to the desktop in folders of each computer. I took them to Office Depot and printed out $450 in pages and put them in 12-pounds of binders and papers. Don noted the files all started oddly on a certain date in 2008 and no data was available on any of them prior to that date. I could have had Don use his data driven brain to decipher the culprits but at this time, I was desperate for normalcy. I had to get back to work and I was running out of the cash and I'm sure he'd like to be paid. I kept the documents and all the backup external drives if I ever needed them for evidence. If bad guys crept back into my life, I could nail them.

I set up a separate Gmail account on a friend's computer so I could communicate with the private detective. I sent him mostly my whereabouts so someone would have account of where I was and also any hard evidence. I was aware that every call rang up $150 hour in fees, but what else was I to do? Maybe "they" would see the e-mail but it would take time to crack the username and password. Everything was about strategy to buy just a little time to make a little progress. I spent countless hours pouring over the recent files which weren't mine and trashed files which weren't mine either. Rick, Sick and / or Bot were having a field day going through my life and pretending it or he or they were me.

WhatIsMyIP.com became an hourly appointment for me to check my computer's IP address to seek clues of the proof of identity of my cyber stalkers. There were lots of other details to the daily data drama that mercifully time has erased from my memory. I gladly turned over the technology security to one smarter than I in that area. I had Don wipe all the devices back to factory settings, some several times under duress, and I bought new Macs.

I unplugged Mac Pro 1, even though it had been completely wiped, and I hadn't used it for an entire year. About two months ago, after Don and normalcy had been with me for nearly half a year, I turned on the original Mac Pro 1 for a freelancer to use. I wondered if that set off the year two, second wave of new cyber scares with the word "efficacious."

Back to last summer, in the Apple stores in three Florida cities, when I asked for help about spyware, they stuck with the corporate-manual mantra, "Macs don't get viruses. Macs don't get spyware. iPhones are safe."

I looked around at the bitten apple logo and as a marketing person wondered what Steve Jobs was thinking when he branded these computers. I looked it up on my iPhone while I waited for the store's salesperson to go into the back room or genius bar to consult with what they call the genius. It's like the Wizard in *Wizard of Oz* where you can't actually see him or her, but someone back there is smarter than all the people buzzing around the stores drinking coffee from Mac mugs and spouting Mac propaganda.

The internet sites told me, "Started 1976 with a sales price of $666.66 ... first logo was of Sir Isaac Newton under an apple tree followed by the bitten apple with rainbow stripes followed by a single color bitten apple ...."

I couldn't come up with the inspiration in my short investigation. It didn't seem to be from Eden with the serpent. I didn't like the repeating sixes in the original price based on my limited knowledge of numerology. My over-thinking and mind overload was interrupted by my gregarious Apple specialist.

"I have all of your products from the back room and will help you load all your software now," she said.

She must have been happy with her voluminous sale. I felt like I bought one of everything in the store. Under all the duress, and with moving the office several times, I couldn't find all my original boxes or serial numbers so I bought all new software, too. I'd just start over, yes, start fresh in every way.

After no life for several months, I had to get back to work. I bought a two-pound Mac Air and a Mac Pro, which I named Mac Pro 2. I'd retire the haunted Mac Pro 1 for a while. I spent hours in the Apple store with their experts setting up the computers for maximum security. I turned on only the most necessary sharing or internet functions. No guest account. Strong password. The Mac Pro 2 would be for production and then I planned to use external drives to move data to the Mac Air for internet functions. I bought Quickbooks for the Mac. Quickbooks was the only program I used on the PC, so I could get rid of that computer altogether. Build barriers. Simplify everything as much as possible. Streamline and fortify. Get back to my life.

I bought the $99 one-year one-on-one package with the new Macs. With an appointment, I could get one-hour of free training or consulting at any Apple store. I found I didn't use it much because I couldn't plan ahead when I might have a question or need assistance. Trekking in and out of the Apple stores, generally located in malls, carrying the weight of up to three computers and iPhones became cumbersome. I bought a collapsible metal grocery cart to put them in, not stylish but back-saving. I tried to use this free service when I could and depended upon the Mac-god, Don, for rock-solid reliable on-the-spot computer consulting. As busy as he was, he could accommodate my emergencies and freak-outs. I bought his $3,000 pay in advance package charged in $150 per hour increments. He was well worth every dollar.

Don and I agreed his time and my money were not great enough for him to resolve the past but move on into the future and prevent and circumvent future issues. Start over.

For nearly a year, I used my new devices without issues and I got back to my life.

CHAPTER 19, LEGAL ADVICE

The boat motor continued the whirring and my own wheels kept spinning in my head about last summer and hoping it wasn't going to be repeated when I hit shore.

Owen's in-house attorney gave me advice that had to be fully implemented now that I had Don in place to help me with the technical side.

The attorney said to send a cease and desist e-mail letter to Rick, since I was certain he was one of the stalkers. I outlined the sequence of events and added the wording that read: "After consulting with professionals, and incurring extensive investment of consulting and legal fees, new phones and computers, I have been advised to not have contact with you in any way including any and all electronic means. So, consider this a formal notice to totally refrain from contacting me or my businesses in any way, including phones and computers, directly or indirectly."

If he violated it, we would then issue a restraining order. If he violated the restraining order, then we could nail him legally for that even if we didn't catch him in cyber crime. I e-mailed the legal notice to him.

I then went on Facebook and un-friended him. I hadn't talked to him in several months, since the phone-borrowing incident. He snapped, and impulsively dialed my office number, which forwarded to my cell, and he left a voice message.

"Hi. I know you have been in Palm Beach a few times and we haven't seen each other. I haven't heard from you. How are things going? Let's get together," he said with his voice shaking.

He obviously hadn't read the email when he left that knee-jerk phone message. That was our last communication, that I'm aware of anyway. After I sent that legal notice, combined with the computer expert sanitizing all my devices, I didn't notice overt spy activity fall, winter, spring, early summer, nothing until right before this July fishing trip.

Now, with conjuring up all the devilish details from a year ago, I added to my mental meltdown, the new word added two days ago to the dictionary word of the day message on the screen that read, "ef.fi.ca.cious Adjective: Successful in producing a desired or intended result; effective. Synonyms: effective – effectual – efficient – operative – potent." The messages from a year ago read, "Attenuate. Wrath. Westering."

I am now totally creeped-out to my core again, just remembering the horror of all in this vivid detail.

CHAPTER 20, SAFE HARBOR WITH BOYFRIEND

"Can you get the lines? Are you alive? We are coming into the marina. It's pretty late. Can you get ready to help with the lines?" Captain was snapping me out of my drift down memory lane.

He was navigating the boat through shallow sharp reefs, where the difference of safe navy blue and catastrophic light teal shallow might be ten-inches apart.

"Are you ever afraid?" I asked.

"No, after 30 years, it's like training a tiger, you learn what not to do. We hit low tide and the currents are rushing but we'll be fine. There is no wind today, so that's good," Captain said.

I was asking about fear in general. Captain's world was his boat, or whatever boat he was captaining at the time, and if it was afloat, why be scared? A marlin could cry beside him and he wouldn't notice.

Captain called on the VHF, "Boat Harbor Marina, Blue Daze we need a slip for the night."

I went downstairs to prepare for docking. We pulled Blue Daze into her slip as the other boaters on the dock were finishing cocktails on their boats, and heading to dinner on the island. On the next dock over, a calypso beat rang out from a sole musician wearing a boat manufacturer logo T-shirt, playing to a small group with a boat sales rep working the crowd. You can see the sales guys across the docks. They wear white pants. They are amped and everyone else is chill-ville.

Before the marina office closed for the day, I raced up to get all of our phones and computers. I wasn't sure for certain if I was supposed to turn mine on or not. I decided to turn my phone on while they got me checked into my hotel room at the marina's hotel property, Abaco Beach Resort.

Owen didn't call, but the e-mail box was loaded and the voice mail on the phone full from Ted.

"I have Sunny on the south dock at Marsh and I'm at Mango's. Call me. If your phone's out, I'll be at the bar waiting for you until sunset. If you get in, I have 8 o'clock reservations for us at Wally's. If you are still out fishing with Owen, you guys be safe and let me know when you'll be back. I'll stay in Marsh the next few days until you get here," said my dear boyfriend Ted in his last voice mail. I didn't check the rest. I wanted to get off the phone quickly.

I checked into the hotel room at Abaco Beach Resort and took a quick splash of a shower. There was never a shower time in the last year where I didn't think of the invasive life-changing scar of a memory. I used to love bubble baths and long, lingering, hot showers. Now showers became perfunctory and I made them as quick as possible. A big downer, and another casualty of the stalker, was Ted and I never had our signature shower sex again. That dried up. Not sex in general, because Ted rocked, but never again in the shower. The cyber creep stole that from us.

Here in the Bahamas, I peeked out of the window overlooking the beach in front and docks to the left. The people below created opaque silhouettes against the harsh perpendicular setting sun. I couldn't wait to see Ted. I had butterflies and got so excited to see him even here in our seventh year. I hurried to get ready and left the room with wet hair. I felt like I was floating down the sidewalk toward the docks. I was happy. I was aware I was happy. I noted that even in total duress, worry and fear, moments of contentedness, and even this joyous moment, can find their way back into a soul. Moments fishing consumed me yesterday where I wasn't totally terrified. This moment now, I am choosing to fill only with love. When I wasn't being suffocated by fear, when I took time to come up for air, there was still a glimmer of myself inside of me. Mentally, I understand to concentrate on the positive, and in most of my life, I practice positive imaging. I am basically a happy person. This spy issue has challenged that practice. I acted, reacted and thought differently living in fear.

At this moment, I felt sense of peace. Looking up into that space, before it became "cyber space," was simply the air above our heads between our wishes and the heavens. In the space of sky and clouds that housed our daydreams, I wished upon the first star as it popped into the sky on the horizon, as I did most nights. I didn't believe stars would grant wishes. Dusk and the presentation of stars simply signaled a point in each day to meditate for a moment, be grateful, and collect thoughts about the day and direction for the future.

I talked to V, my little inner voice, or inner guidance, which for me is God. On this night, I asked V strength to continue the cyber battle or wisdom to waive the white flag.

I heard V clearly in my head, "You have the protection of the wings of one-thousand angels. Look up. Protecting them are one-thousand more for every star of the sky."

A huge flock of seagulls was resting on the beachfront by the resort, and they all in unison picked up from their restful state and rose into the heavens flapping their wings of white.

V's responses often might be a word or phrase. I pulled out the ever-present pen and pad of paper in my purse and wrote this message down to be sure to remember it exactly as said. I would share it with Ted later. He would be pleased to hear this. I would tell Owen, too. It made me feel a sense of relief about Owen's welfare in Bimini or wherever he was now. The message gave me an inner peace and I felt a gentle chill melt down me, starting at the top of my head, like a trickle of water under a gentle waterfall.

I was acutely aware that in this moment, my thoughts, like my words, were flowing in peaceful, spiritual, philosophical waves. I was generally centered in this mindset, but the fear and suspicion of the last year bathed my peace in an itchy, annoying, irritating, unresolved chicken-pox-style mental state.

I packed for this Bahamas trip so quickly, that I didn't have a dinner dress. Men like to fish with tomboys but on date night, no matter how much they say it doesn't matter, they want you pink and soft. Cotton resort wear would do so I walked from the marina a few blocks across to the bay and into the boutique at Wally's and found a Lilly bright pink halter top dress with lime green palm trees and turquoise cocoanuts. "Theme night," I thought, "Let's go back to the days of cocoanut telephones and communicate with simplicity. Digital detox here we come."

The sun was setting and the 100-degree weather was cooling to a balmy 85-degrees and the breeze picked up to 15 knots, cooling my sunburned face. I'm normally tenacious about sunscreen but with all the distractions, missed that step in the day's routine. As I was walking across the street to Mango's, Ted was coming towards me. "I love this man," I thought. We greeted each other with a tender embrace and I clung to him trying to keep this very moment alive forever.

"You really missed me didn't you?" he asked in response to my atypical clinginess.

"You have no idea!" I exclaimed.

We sauntered across the street to our favorite corner table at Wally's, on the porch of the pink Victorian villa.

"We had a bite on and boated 25 fish today. The guys are stoked and signed up for the next tournament with me," beamed Ted.

"I'll have the Wally's Special," I told the server deciding early on that several rums and fruit juices were preferable to any diet or Grey Goose anything, "Bring on the cracked conch and the fun, then whatever chef's special is today."

I wanted to spend my time immersed in my man and not in a menu. The filet mignon, lamb chops, smothered grouper were all delicious and there was not a bad choice on the menu. A romantic dinner listening to the live acoustic guitar and vocalist soothed the soul and Ted's cheerful chatter about his week, his day, and his guy-land friends all lifted my spirits. I was working hard to be in this moment, and be positive, and be happy. If V promised we would be safe, then we would. I played V's message in my mind, in the background of the conversation with Ted.

"Maybe we can just move here," I pleaded playfully after two more of the libations.

"To Marsh Harbour? We practically live here already. We're here all the time," said Ted.

"Then it will be an easy transition. Let's look at some of the bungalows between Pete's Pub and the Ritz tomorrow," I continued.

"Sure, they'd be good rentals during season," said Ted the indulgent playmate, but always the consummate businessman.

I was thinking maybe really move from Florida to the islands for a while. If Owen's maximum threat came to pass, who knew what was going to happen in the U.S. in the next few weeks. Here in the Bahamas, their electricity goes out all the time, but you don't care because you have a generator on the boat and you are in a swimsuit catching fish for dinner anyway. Back home, oil, electricity and energy feed the machine.

I didn't burden Ted with any of the negativity swelling back into my life, partially for his sake, but mostly for mine. We endured last summer and had months of peaceful, normal life. I wanted the ultimate escapism of wining, dining and dating. I'm a romantic through and through and the seduction starts with the first breathy kiss and ends with the dark of our room waiting for us at the Abaco Beach Resort. Darkness incarnate and his evil doings could wait till tomorrow to make itself known to Ted.

We left Bay Street to go back to Sand Bar at the marina with a live Bahamian band singing something like, "That old guy's no good for you, don't you want some of this..."

There were tipsy tourists flirting with Bahamian men on the pool-side dance floor getting some of that. Captain had a cute redhead gyrating with him and singing her lungs out. She knew the lyrics to the local island tunes so she must have island-hopped some to learn all those words. I joined my own man to cut a rug to a few island favorite tunes.

The bar was packed. The end of the summer sailboat regatta, with over 300 sailboats, was descending upon Marsh Harbour the next day, and some early birds had made their way in already. We missed the naked party at Fiddler's Key, and the one at Guana's famous bar, Nippers. The full moon party at Cracker P's in Hope Town was the chatter for the next evening.

We had a few rounds with Captain and the redhead. We said our good-nights and retired to our room for private time, less the shower sex.

CHAPTER 21, TURTLES ARE PROTECTED

We woke early. The curse of two morning people is that no matter how late you stay up the night before, you'll wake up with the roosters. The wild chickens and roosters running around in the bushes called to us.

We hopped on Ted's boat Sunny for a morning cruise and coffee a la sunrise, and set out for the National Park by Pete's Pub to snorkel for an hour. On the boat ride, I filled Ted in on the predicament of Owen and our precarious futures. I told him I feared the demon might be trying to re-enter our lives. He didn't respond much. I was happy to don the snorkel gear and hop into the water with masks where we couldn't talk.

Ted pointed out a turtle, neither a baby like I've seen crawling from nests to the ocean, nor a giant adult like I've seen floating in the ocean, but maybe a "preschooler" I speculated. He was stunning with bright yellow markings. He wasn't afraid of us and cocked his head and stretched his neck towards us in curiosity as we swam closer to him. On the reef behind him, in a crevice, I could see something he should be afraid of, a poisonous lionfish. The venomous spikes of the lionfish prevented predators from nearing him and here in the Caribbean and in the waters surrounding Florida, the lionfish have no natural predators, other than an occasional lionfish derby organized by marine protectors. The naive turtle with his protective shell was a victim in the waiting for the prickly predator, like us normal people doing normal daily tasks to the cyber stalkers. I wondered if I would ever escape fully from my stalker, if I could ever look at nature and not see him in the spiny one, if I could talk to my boyfriend for more than an hour or two without bringing up the topic.

We climbed back into the boat, dried off some and I tied a white lacy beach cover over my swimsuit. We pulled into Little Harbour by Pete's Pub. A tour bus had made it through the pot-holed one lane sand roads from the Ritz property Winding Bay and four tourists were joining the locals who already had congregated in the primo Adirondack chairs near the fans. All the seats were outside with a boat turned bar as the focal point. A sweaty bartender offered a smile, a warm greeting and an ice cold Blaster, the house drink of rums and fruit juices. I opted for a Diet Coke and Pete's famous fish sandwich.

Our Bahamian Captain friend was winning at the ring toss game. I could never remember his real name but I called him Frack. He was like Frick and Frack with Captain Ed when we were in Marsh Harbour.

"Where's my man Captain Ed?" Frack asked and gave Ted and me each a huge smile and a big Bahamian hug.

"We've got a noon call to Owen on the boat. We just dropped in for a quick early lunch bite. We just saw the cutest turtle on the reef. I've never seen one so unafraid and just maybe ten-inches wide," I answered.

"Bahamians like to eat turtles, but now you spend a year in jail if you are caught. Turtles come right up to the shore here at Pete's all the time. They won't get hurt because they are protected," said Frack.

"I'd like to be a little turtle protected on this slice of paradise. I'd just pull in my head and arms and legs and know I didn't have to worry about anything, that I was protected," I considered, looking down, and glanced back at Frack who was quite confused by my ponderings.

"How do Bahamians see the marlin? Do they need any protection? Are they endangered?" I had never asked before.

"Oh, the blue marlin are deep water fish and love the Abacos especially Cherokee Point in Cherokee Sound here by Pete's. If you fish a few days here, you are guaranteed to catch a marlin and sailfish, too. Out of 37 boats in the tournament last week, every single boat caught at least one marlin," reported Frack.

"Of course the marlin are fine," I thought, "Captains from Florida or the Caribbean think if they are still swimming around they must be just fine."

I thought of how unaware the captains were of the plight of the boat owners, the marlins, and as long as the Kalik flowed and the fuel flowed in the tank, all is good in the world.

"I won $400 plus a big bar tab last night at ring toss at Curly Tails. A mega yacht guy said he'd give me $400 if I got three out of five, so I got five out of five, and he gave me $500 so I could cover the bar tab, too," chuckled Frack.

Life is a game to Bahamians and win or lose, it's always win, because you live here doing this. Life is good.

"Ready for the chick challenge?" he asked.

"Sure," I agreed as I grabbed the silver ring tied to the string hung from the tree above and aimed it with great precision at the hook on the tree trunk. I released it to grab the hook on the first try.

"Woo-hoo. Girlfriend is hot. You go Charlotte," cheered Frack.

He let me aim directly at the hook as a handicap. He flung his sideways wrapping it multiple times around a pole, then it would glide over and at least half the time gracefully land on the hook. He put on a show of skill and showmanship. He made me laugh. His lighthearted spirit, and his much greater score by the time our lunch was served, lightened my cash to buy his lunch. I ordered lunch, but couldn't eat much of it in nervous anticipation of the pending phone call to Owen.

CHAPTER 22, MARLIN BATTLE CRY

Ted and I met Captain on Owen's boat Blue Daze at 11:45 a.m. for the noon call to Owen. The TV was on. The TV was always on with Captain around, just like when I had my teens at home. You can walk down the docks at all times of the day and night and see the flicker of monitors inside the boats. I don't care for TV, but captains like it I assume to create some privacy with background noise and to stay connected to the outside world.

The outside world's TV commercials were for a GM car with a voice activated computer, Magic Jack and iPhone's Siri service. The TV flashed a teaser for the noon news, "Another star stays away from the red carpet because of a Tweeted threat to her life. A deranged fan believes her Tweets are directly to him and that they have a relationship and he's jealous of her star boyfriend. Stay tuned for the whole story."

"Why can't we trace the thumb finger prints of the creep behind those Tweets?" I snarled at the TV. "We need Corporate America or government to give us the technology to identify criminals online. Then citizens can go through existing authorities and proper chan-nels already in place to prosecute bad behavior. Just as if we had a burglar, we would identify them. We don't need big brother to monitor our communications, only evolve the communication tech-nology so creepy behavior is in the public, not hidden in a coward-ice corner. A peeping Tom can be identified, then can be charged and prosecuted. A criminal, who enters your home and threatens you, confronts your legal right to shoot him dead. Let's bring these cyber cowards into the light of day. I hope we get a solution soon. For all of our sakes," I continued.

Captain said, "You get too riled up about things that don't con-cern you. Who cares about that Hollywood chick and her red carpet? I might have to deal with the boat right under us being sold. Keep your feet on the ground, on what is important."

He clicked off the TV and we all sat silent for a moment in the salon of the Hatteras in an awkward nervous anticipation.

"I have Owen's phone here so I don't know how he'll answer it, unless he can answer on another line," I pointed out, "Maybe he'll call us. We'll be here together to get out next instructions anyway."

95

I dialed Owen's number using the speakerphone option on my iPhone. His flip phone on the boat sat silent and turned off as directed, and we could hear on our end that it rang elsewhere.

"Hello, Team Blue," cheerfully greeted Owen, "This Old-School Marlin has positive news for you. Turn on the Palm Beach CBS noon news then call me back. We'll talk more in a few minutes. Bye for now."

His cheerful greeting immediately lightened the thick air in the room. I felt oxygen in my lungs.

Captain turned back on the TV and turned up the volume. A get-rich-quick personal injury commercial aired. A plastic surgery commercial aired. A heated political commercial aired. The newscaster showed video of Owen's company's Gulf oil spill with a breaking story, "Yesterday in a quiet transfer, American Valor Company bought the leaking oil rig in the Gulf of Mexico off the Florida coast. With new technology developed by conglomerate American Valor, they stopped the leak this morning. American Valor is implementing break-through technology in the oil clean up. The US-based technology and energy giant American Valor bought the rig to use as the base for their ocean ecology research lab."

Owen was interviewed on the Louisiana beach with the president of American Valor, "We had a pending sale fall through and our long-time friends at American Valor Company stepped in with a partnership offer and a miraculous solution to the oil leak."

"This is a miracle. How does he accomplish these things?" I marveled.

"He's always buying and selling businesses. I don't even try to keep up with his list of investments. If there is news about the oil industry, he generally is involved. The guy makes some serious bucks. When he's here on the boat, we're all wearing the same Blue Daze T-shirts. He leaves that TV persona on shore and he's a regular guy. Hey, think Owen will keep the boat now?" asked Captain.

"Let's call!" I suggested and hit the redial button on speakerphone.

"The Mexicans are out. Truly out entirely, not just out of my oil company, out of our lives. We took care of them. So, last summer your unprotected PC gave the Mexicans access. They found the

96

marketing plan files on your Mac through the PC on your network. The Billionaire-Bot looked for anything with a U.S. dollar sign and more than 10 digits. That activity showed up on your Mac last summer when my CIA associate set up diagnostics for you. We've been dealing with them ever since, and it really came down to the wire this time. So, we orchestrated the sale to American Valor, cash is flowing, not oil, so let's reorganize Team Blue now," said Owen.

"Charlotte, I need you in New Orleans Wednesday to create the national PR splash for the oil clean up effort. We'll fish next weekend and revisit the marketing plan since we are keeping the oil company this year. And, by the way, your computer problems have been wiped from your devices and from the face of the earth. We handled that as part of our arrangement. You can watch the CBS evening news for that report," said Owen as he addressed me.

I didn't ask for details about how he handled Rick and Sick and Bot. I really didn't hate any of them, didn't know the people behind the Bot, and didn't wish them any harm although I'm quite sure serious harm of one kind or another came their way. At this point, I just wanted them out of my life and they were finally.

"Hey Ted, back at ya', right? Remember the Poltergeist's message of 'efficacious: successful in producing a desired or intended result; effective.' Remember?" I whispered to Ted and he cracked up in a big exhale of relief.

"Efficacious describes the successful and effective you, not creep-boy Rick," smugly agreed Ted in a whisper back.

"Captain, cruise Blue Daze to Punta Cana by Saturday; I hear the blue marlin are running in the Dominican. Ted, join us if you like. I'm back online with phone working if you need me. Let's get back to play today and work Monday," said Owen.

So the marlin didn't die, he just cried a little, and the salty tears made him stronger and determined. The tears kept him alive. He made a battle cry to the other marlins to unite to defend their honor, their wealth, and their businesses against the evil electronic enemy. Marlin-man Owen was back stronger than ever. He wasn't selling his businesses, or his boat. He was still a marlin migrating, and hunting, and being big and mighty, and ruling the high seas.

He was a marlin back to doing what marlins do.

CHAPTER 23, GOOD NEWS ABOUT A REALLY BAD GUY

Ted, Captain and I took the Contender Sunny out to Cherokee and brought back four dolphin. Ted's answer for glory or defeat is always, "Let's wet a line."

"This light drizzle can't dampen my spirits. A hurricane couldn't faze me today. I'm on Cloud Nine," I announced to the guys.

"You're looking better already. You were getting old fast sister. Nothing is worth that stress. You could have replaced all that tech anchor you carry around with all the income you would have made if you had been billing hours instead of being paranoid. Just throw that computer junk in the shipwreck graveyard if that happens again," said Captain.

"My girl is surfing glassies with me on surfboards and boats, not surfing the net for spyware lingo. Never again. It robbed us of several months," piped in Ted.

We all met at Blue Daze at 6 p.m. to watch the Palm Beach CBS affiliate news. I couldn't sit. I paced back and forth in the ten-foot wide salon area. At 6:20 p.m. the news we were waiting for broke, "Live from West Palm Beach, authorities have arrested alleged cyber criminal Andrick "Rick" Kira, and seized his arsenal of star stalker electronics. He was traced to his home from a sexual stalker Tweet he sent to singing star Cheyenne. The trace was possible by using new technology developed by American Valor Company. Candid photos, allegedly shot by serial stalker Andrick, of Cheyenne, and 35 other women of all ages, about half of whom are stars and public figures, are taped all over his walls, with hand-written messages on Post-it notes that authorities are describing as 'disturbing.' The concert for Cheyenne in the Cruzan Ampitheatre will continue as scheduled this evening. Read more about this breaking news story on our station website."

"Wooo-hoo! Go Owen! He nailed your stalker guy. Owen rocks," cheered Captain.

"See! I told you all along I wasn't paranoid. You deal with sharks you can see. My cyber sharks were just as scary but chewed through the wires and popped out of my monitor into my lap! I wonder what my Post-it note said if he had my photo hung on his stalker wall?" I asked.

"I'm putting a Post-It note on you now that says, 'She's free!' so let's celebrate," said Ted.

"You know, of my terror trio, Bot down, Rick down, that still leaves Sick," I sighed.

"Let him off the hook this time. If it's who we think it is, and we are 95 percent sure we know, you won't hear a peep from that guy. He's going to fade back into the background so fast. He's a business guy. He watches the news and sees the witch hunt Owen is on now. He's not insane enough at this point to make himself a vulnerable target for a legal battle. It would ruin his career, his reputation and his whole life. With you, I doubt he'll ever rear his ugly head again. If he does, I have a quick fix planned," assured Ted.

"You know when the authorities start investigating Rick's bounty of data, they are going to find embarrassing photos and videos of people," I gingerly presented a hint at our sex films in Rick's possession.

"I thought of that a year ago when it happened. The bad guys aren't the only ones with access to technology. It took some serious work, research, and dollar bills, but I infiltrated Rick's computers through his massive security system. I isolated the files with the films of us and destroyed them. The films no longer exist," beamed Ted.

"Ha! The Boogeyman is no match for my man! But, that is weird. Why didn't you tell me you were spying on Rick?" I responded.

"You were worried enough. I wanted you, and still want you, to put all this drama behind us in the past where it belongs," said Ted.

"I bet a tidal wave of serious fear just hit New York City and Palm Beach Island where Rick had all of his cyber security clients. He was supposedly providing security for entire estates in the millions and millions of dollars. The drama for him, and them, is just starting," I said.

CHAPTER 24, LIGHT AT FIREFLY

We left the door to Blue Daze unlocked. You can do that in most of the islands. We walked to Sand Bar by the marina pool for happy hour. Captain and the redhead left to join Bahamian Captain friend Frack who was playing traditional Bahamian musical instruments, the butter knife and a saw, in a rake and shake band at Snappas on Bay Street.

Ted and I strolled back down the dock reading the names on the backs of the boats and guessed whom the owners might be. In boating life, you often resort to non-electronic entertainment such as curly tail races, joke telling, story telling, sometimes games such as Pictionary or Trivial Pursuit, but mostly chilling and conversation. The tide of normal life was flowing back in and soothing our scorched souls.

"Snap Crackle, that's got to be a cereal family," guessed Ted about a mega yacht.

Our next neighbor on the dock was a floating condo looking vessel where the people attached what looked like all their earthly belongings to the sides and top. I guessed, "The Grape Escape so maybe they owned a vineyard or they like wine?"

A shiny black go-fast boat Ted laughed, "Flesh On? Now this must be a dancer bar owner or something."

We hopped in his boat Sunny for a one-Kalik relaxing ride to the new Firefly Bar and Grill overlooking the Sea of Abaco for a stunning purple sunset. Ted liked the Firefly Sweet Tea Vodka cocktail and I liked the Firefly Skinny Tea Vodka cocktail made with Crystal Light. The resort with tin roof cottages dotted up the hill, was situated between Hope Town Lodge and the Abaco Inn, with little in between. We toasted a successful day and gratitude for a perfect evening. We ordered fish tacos and mingled with the small crowd.

The TV was on in the top corner of the bar tucked beside the vast bottles of vodkas and rums. We overheard comments on the Gulf oil spill from a yacht crew all dressed in matching teal T-shirts sitting across the bar. Boaters are passionate about the sea. One exclaimed, "Man, I'm glad they are mopping up that oil mess. I'm from Orange Beach in the Panhandle and we just recovered from

101

the last oil rig slickster slip up."

Another chimed in, "Yeah, the big dogs don't care about the fish or us fishermen. They only care about banking big daddy bucks and they muck up our world in the process."

I whispered to Ted, "I have a big PR job ahead of me. Listen to these guys. Where do they think the $30,000 a month comes from to fuel that big yacht they live on? I wonder if they realize that one of the marlins, the big dogs, has to provide us with oil, all these yachts, the marinas, and provide most of us with the opportunity to earn a living doing what we love. Even more, given the events of the last few days, I wonder if they ever consider what the marlin goes through to keep everything afloat, literally. I saw a marlin cry this week."

"The boating world is a severe micro-peek at haves and have-nots peacefully prospering together. The boat owners create wealth then join in the fun when they can with the captains, mates, cooks, bikini contest girls, and islanders, who all benefit from the cash flowing. People-watching here, or anywhere really, gives me more insights than any marketing research focus group in Florida ever has," I added.

He said, "You've worked enough this week. Let's have fun and tip a few."

I responded, "I love what I do. I'll be just one little firefly light in the world, one little light. This is fun to me to listen to them and try to figure out how to communicate with them. The marlins aren't the bad guys. We need leaders to continue to create and nurture opportunities for all of us, and people to lead at all levels of society to protect our culture. The beauty of red, white and blue in free America is that any of us can be leaders. We live in capitalistic America. I've already started writing Owen's speech in my head."

On the way home, we boated past the full moon party at Cracker P's, with a few hundred partiers converging on the docks. Floating across the glassy water, over the boat's engine, you could hear the rhythmic beat of heavy island percussion backed with keyboard and bass. We motored up closer to shore and could see the rake and scrape saws, goatskin drums, maracas, and cow bells. The vocals sang of mangos and the moon.

The gravity of the full moon and the band at Sand Bar seduced us back towards our dock space. We turned Sunny towards Boat Harbor where we had our own howl-at-the-moon party planned with each other.

Sunday I recall very little of what we did which is a good sign that life was again as it should be; digital detox fully in effect and replaced with deliriously positive island life intoxication. I changed my password on my iPhone to "Yippee!!DINGdong2day." I sang, "Ding, dong the witch is dead," from *Wizard of Oz*. I sang it in the shower. I indulged in a long, hot, steamy shower as I bid farewell to fear and gloom. I got my voice back, my inner voice. In my head played Elton John's *Someone Saved My Life Tonight* lyrics, "Sweet freedom whispered in my ear..." The song was said to have been written at an extreme low point for Elton John, and we all know what happened from there with his career; the high point of success!

Ted joined me in the shower and sang to me Tim McGraw's *I Know How To Love You Well*, "I may not be the best of singers, There's better guys I've heard, But I know how to love, I know how to love you well."

I was back. We were back. My life was coming back.

CHAPTER 25, HOME TO CIVILIZED SOCIETY

On the way home to the civilized society of America, the small Beechcraft hit turbulence, as a strong front was moving in. Hurricane season was brewing at sea right on cue. I waited a few minutes for the plane to push through the bouncing and began writing again. My pen propelled itself across the blue lined pad of paper always tucked in my pirate beach bag.

I read my written thought to Ted in the seat across from me, "Violent storms massacring the shores reveal hidden dangers and secrets. On a beach walk one day, you might find solitude and inspiration. Following a storm, you might find rare shells or valuable treasures. You might also have to maneuver past shards of glass, the stench of trash or piles of driftwood forcing you to make a choice to go under, go around or turn around. In life, storms are as necessary as they are in nature. Storms reveal to us our barriers, show us sharp objects, and make obvious and clear the safe passage."

"You are such a film producer. Everything to you is a story line or prose isn't it?" he laughed.

"I'm a writer. I see life as a potential screenplay. You have been cast as my male muse," I playfully confirmed.

I flipped the paper and continued my notes in preparation for the Dominican Republic trip, "Proposal for Project DR Green-Care at the Super Scooter Manufacturing Plant: Create global goodwill by recycling island blight. Take the roadways and expansive fields littered with trash and auto graveyards and create a recycling program. Implement a financial incentive for citizens to bring trash to a large truck recycling mobile-facility in each community village center, rather than dumping garbage randomly all over their island. The islanders will associate the branded trucks with income for themselves, when they see trucks in their community, and as trucks transport the trash to a central facility. Create a simple manufacturing facility that produces a creative reinvention of the trash into modular sheets of metal roof panels, modular plastic wall panels and modular glass windows. Through creative reinvention, make blight beautiful and purposeful!"

I handed the pad to Ted and said, "Hey, read this. Remember last year I suggested we recycle the trash into public art, but that island, as many island nations do, could use practical products instead. They will agree to let us set up this infrastructure as part of the Super Scooter manufacturing plant on the island. You and Owen have your joint project in the DR. The scooters will provide afford-able transportation for the islanders and a profitable export item. Dominicans pack four and five people on scooters in the villages now and wreck all the time. Your affordable scooters will save lives there because they can ride with one or two people, not a whole family. The job creation and exportation will give the Dominicans opportunity for income to purchase the scooters. I'll create positive PR for the DR citizens, and also internationally as you export the Super Scooters. It's a great win-win."

"I can see your creative juices are flowing again. I like that your ideas are flowing without being attached to anything electronic," Ted said.

"My messages aren't necessarily created using electronics, but they end up on TV, film, radio, or internet. Everything I do is connected somehow to the electronic world. My generic word for computers, 'Macs,' isn't a bad word. Computers are awesome. Some people are bad; it's that simple. I'm excited to work on creative solutions for grounded, earthy issues like oil spills and recycling, not chasing vaporous vampires with flashlights. I'm so relieved to free my brain cells for positive thoughts and be back in the flow of my life. I wish there were ten of me; there are so many things I want to do! I had to give up our extended romantic getaway and my writing sabbatical this trip, but it's the nature of doing crisis-management PR to be flexible," I said.

"As for our vampire Rick, or Andrick, he told me his name in Rus-sian means 'warrior' but looks like the warrior lost this battle. As for Captain, in this adventure, he wasn't very supportive. He didn't even want to hear about the cyber mess," I complained.

"It's not his fault. It's who he is. The boat is his whole world. I read in *Forbes* lately that captains are in a top profession to make six figures. Interesting, right? But many of them have the mental outlook of working class citizens. It could be because the boat owners make so much more than six figures so in the boating world, captains are on bottom, not on top of income level. In reality, Americans represent the top three percent of the world's wealth; we are all wealthy individuals compared to citizens of many other nations. Regardless of income, cyber security is never going to be Captain's big quest of the day, where the fish are biting will be the only concern. Give him a break. He lives in a bubble, but look at you, too. You are obsessed by your work and your life. Most of us are busy living our lives and not concerned about the world. 'The world' is too big of a concept for most of us," observed Ted, making quote signs with his fingers.

"And then there is Owen. You know when Captain pulls the marlin from the water to release the circle hook and the fish is so close that you can smell death on his breath? You know that look a marlin gives you, after a long battle with the rod, and he looks you right in the eye mano-a-mano wondering if at that moment if he will live or die? You know, when the big fish wonders if he has been overpowered and his demise is upon him? When he has given up? Owen had that look. Owen cried. The marlin cried," I said.

"Even the mighty face peril and damnation at times. None of us can feel too superior or experience genuine safety. History tells us tides change. We've travelled ourselves to ruins of mighty civilizations in Machu Picchu, Rome, Egypt, Buenos Aires, China, and all over. The citizens of civilizations are always in constant battle to protect the characteristics and values that define them. Well, the big marlin, Owen, turned the red tide this time and saved all the fish. He overcame the hostile takeover and cyber espionage of his companies, and presumably halted the more widespread devastating national threats. What would have happened if Owen and the Secret Service had not blocked the threats?" asked Ted.

"My tidal wave vision," I whispered to myself.

"Your what?" he asked.

"It's a long story. I'll tell you later," I said.

Neither Ted nor Owen was intuitive, but they both indulged me in sharing. They both showed interest in and validated my insights. I decided I would tell Ted about my recurring vision, but later.

"You will finish your happy rainbow promises book now, right?" asked Ted, changing the subject, assuming his performance was next in the review process following Owen and Captain Ed.

"Yes! This cyber scare gave me the dark chapter. It was a gift, really. Life is how you think about it. Every book needs the antagonist, doesn't it? I still believe 'life is good' and will continue to fully live my life in that way. I had planned to stay in the Bahamas and write, but I can write anywhere in the world, even here and now! I must write. Nothing will stop me," I confirmed.

With that declaration, as if on cue on a film set, the turbulence stopped altogether, and a sunbeam brightened the cozy passenger cabin. I peered outside the oval window and, at eye level, saw a hint of a rainbow in the atmosphere next to the raincloud beside me. The sapphire ring on my left hand, reflected the beam, crowning the ceiling over our heads with a soothing blue hue. On my right hand, my emerald ring, encircled and flanked by tiny diamonds embedded into the platinum, caught the light and formed a cocoon of a thousand tiny dancing flickers surrounding us.

The floating sparkles reminded me of V's promise at sunset on the beach. I pointed up to the lights, and I reminded Ted, "You have the protection of the wings of one-thousand angels. Look up. Protecting them are one-thousand more for every star of the sky."

"This finally all makes sense! Words have power. Instead of giving into messages that communicated like a threat, we stopped (attenuate) evil (wrath) from coming to the west (westering.) Get it? By having faith and listening, we got promises. Words do have power. Words, and His Promises, are powerful (efficacious,)" I surmised out loud, as my whole body filled with chills.

I smiled and reflectively reminded myself who I was in this life, "My life's destiny was to be a writer. I've always known what I was to be. In recent years, I prepared for my children's college years as my own time to get a quiet beach place to write, run my company remotely from a laptop, and travel the world experiencing coastlines and cultures. My destiny was to write and publish books, and produce films, exploring the human spirit to help heal the tender spots of humanity."

The End. (For Now.)

AUTHOR'S NOTE

9/17/12 as I write my final edit, the fictional main character, and I, Casey the real writer and real person who experienced the computer monitor messages, "got it." I wrote one more paragraph into the story and added a page to the book.

I wrote this for the book, and also for healing for myself:
"This finally all makes sense! Words have power. Instead of giving into what communicated like a threat, we stopped (attenuate) evil (wrath) from coming to the west (westering.) Get it? By having faith and listening, we got promises. Words do have power. Words, and His Promises, are powerful (efficacious,)" I surmised out loud.

ALSO, in real life, it rains most afternoons in Florida, thus, we have abundant rainbows daily. Rainbows are not unusual in the Sunshine State. Today, as I added the above paragraph as my final entry for this book, six friends on Facebook posted candid photos of a unique giant rainbow spanning all of Orlando. I now feel confident that this book is complete and ready for press. I'll start work again on the real rainbow book now!